Goodbye, My Irish Child

by Monica McCormack-Sheehan

PublishAmerica
Baltimore

© 2004 by Monica McCormack-Sheehan.
All rights reserved. No part of this book may be reproduced, stored in a retrieval system or transmitted in any form or by any means without the prior written permission of the publishers, except by a reviewer who may quote brief passages in a review to be printed in a newspaper, magazine or journal.

First printing

ISBN: 1-4137-1989-9
PUBLISHED BY PUBLISHAMERICA, LLLP
www.publishamerica.com
Baltimore

Printed in the United States of America

I dedicate this book to my inner child.
11-12-05

Dear Anne,

Life is a journey and this book tells a small part of my journey. Hope you enjoy it.

Slán go fóil.

Love,
Monica M. Sheehan.

Acknowledgments

Special thanks to my teachers and mentors, Jim and Sherry Husfelt, who showed me how to heal the wounds of my soul and give my inner child back her voice; and to my dear friends and spiritual warriors who are shining beacons in this time of darkness: Rachael Kain, Janet Rudolph, Andrea Mroz, Jane Justice, Mark Speranza, Phil Salem, Alfred Darby, Jim Kalnins, and Rick Liberty.

To my husband Jim and three beautiful children, Grace, Emma and Sarah, for all their patience, love and encouragement. To my wonderful friend, Gerri Snyder, for her labour of love in editing.

To Gerard McCormac for helping me to reconnect with the essence of Ireland, and for encouraging me to express my Irishness.

This book would not be possible without my parents, John and Teresa McCormack, who gave me life and the freedom to live it; the McCormack gang—Kathleen, Mary, Skip, Grace, Michael, and Covey; and to all the lads from the neighbourhood.

My love and gratitude to ye all.

A Word to the Reader

As Mark Twain once said, "I find that the further back I go, the better I remember things, whether they happened or not!"

These are my memories as I recall them. They are true insofar as I remember them, but then all literature is invention. Two people standing together, witnessing the very same scene, will remember it differently. Such is the nature of memory. It is very selective. Each event did take place, though not necessarily in the manner recounted. Some readers may consider this a work of fiction and that cannot be helped, as oftentimes truth is stranger than fiction. Names have been changed to protect the innocent and the guilty.

Table of Contents

Chapter One
Free at Last..17

Chapter Two
The Setting...28

Chapter Three
Bonfire Night..35

Chapter Four
My Own Bike at Last.................................40

Chapter Five
A Cycle to Ballybunnion...........................45

Chapter Six
The Graveyard Dare..................................57

Chapter Seven
Adventures in Cow Dung.........................66

Chapter Eight
The West Clare Railway..................................76

Chapter Nine
Deep Water..90

Chapter Ten
Relieve You...98

Chapter Eleven
Cappa..105

Chapter Twelve
The Fields..113

Chapter Thirteen
Rawkin' Apples..120

Epilogue
Dropping the Stone..133

Remembrance of Home

Have you ever been to the West of Clare
And seen the bogs and rocky land,
Felt the breeze that lingers there,
Or held its wildflowers in your hand?

Have you walked through miles of countryside
Down winding roads and over hills,
Watched the rabbits run and hide,
Or dropped some coins in the holy wells?

Have you stood in awe upon its cliffs
And watched the waves in motion,
Been wet by spray or drizzly mists
That sweep in from the ocean?

Have you seen the hay so neatly piled
And the cattle gently grazing,
Smelt the gorse that's growing wild
In a day that's warm and hazy?

As the cattle sit and chew the cud
You sigh and long to stay.
If all were well you surely would,
But you have to go away.

By Monica McCormack

CLARE
ENNIS
KILRUSH
Cill Rois
KILKEE
Cill Chaoi
TARBERT
BALLYLONGFORD
BALLYBUNNION
FOYNES
RATHKE

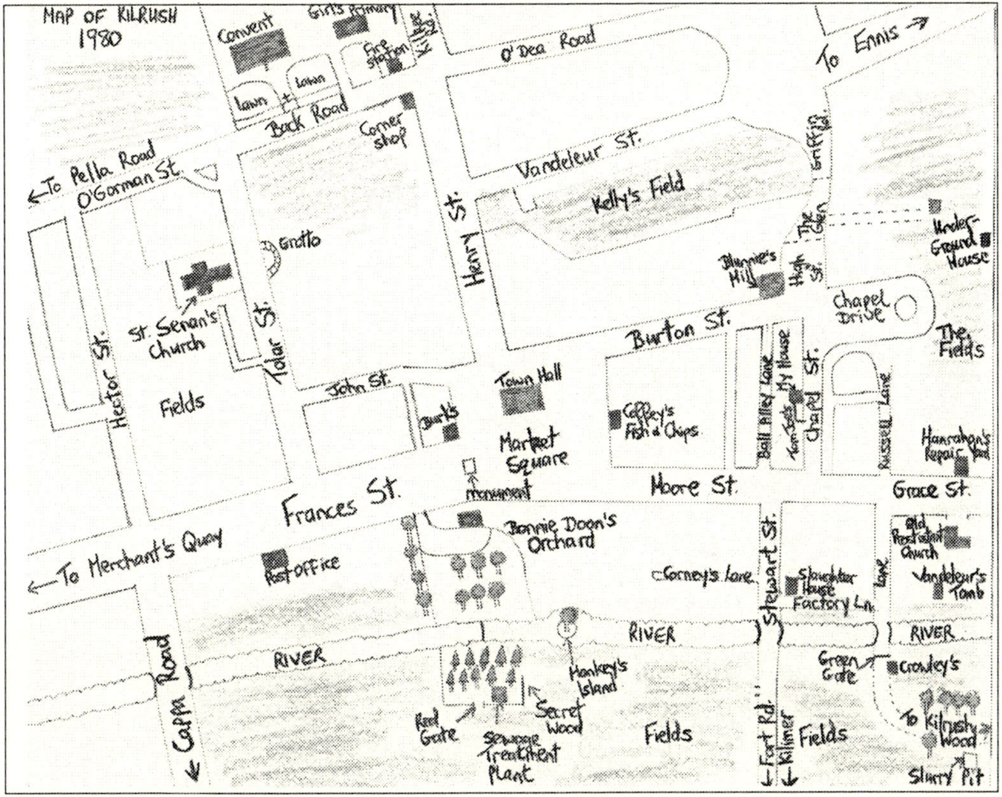
MAP OF KILRUSH
1980
Convent
Girls Primary
Fire station
Lawn
Lawn
Back Road
O'Dea Road
To Ennis
←To Pella Road
O'Gorman St.
Corner shop
Vandeleur St.
Kelly's Field
Griffin St.
The Glen
Under-Ground House
Grotto
Henry St.
Mill
High St.
Chapel Drive
The Fields
St. Senan's Church
Tolar St.
Hector St.
Burton St.
Fields
John St.
Town Hall
Market Square
Ball Alley Lane
My House
Chapel St.
Russell Lane
Fish & Chips
Hanrahan's Repair Yard
Monument
Frances St.
Moore St.
Grace St.
Bonnie Doon's Orchard
Old Protestant Church
←To Merchant's Quay
Post office
Corney's Lane
Stewart St.
Slaughter House
Factory Ln.
Lane
Vandeleur's Tomb
RIVER
RIVER
RIVER
Road
Hankey's Island
Green Gate
Crowley's
Secret Wood
Red Gate
Sewage Treatment Plant
Fields
Fort Rd.
Kilimer
Fields
To Kilrush Wood
Slurry Pit

Chapter One
Free At Last

The final bell rang. With a loud crash, the doors were thrown open and out poured hundreds of wild, excited, free children. School bags were tossed up in the air, jumped on, or kicked back and forth like footballs. Notebooks were ripped to shreds, tossed in glee overhead and came floating back down like a tickertape parade. The scraps made a mess on the playground, which the children ignored. They were free at last. Two and a half months of no school, no homework, but all fun and games were stretched before them like a long-anticipated birthday party.

As for me, I slowly rose from my desk at the back of the classroom. I had been exiled there six months previously for not learning a page by heart from my Irish language textbook. I've never forgotten that day. I was sitting in the front of the classroom then, right next to Sr. Benedict's desk, when she asked me to stand up and recite my Irish homework. I always thought that learning a page of Irish by heart was a waste of time and didn't put too much effort into it. If I had known the penalty for such folly, maybe I would have applied myself with a little more diligence. Needless to say, I was unable to give the performance desired and, as a punishment, was sent to the back of the classroom, never to be taught again. I was forbidden to ask questions, and when I handed in an assignment or test it was given back to me unmarked. This was so typical of my years in primary school that I ceased to argue and just accepted my punishment with resignation.

At four years old, I had entered the institution of education at the Mercy School in my hometown—Kilrush, West Clare, on the west coast of Ireland. It was a school for girls taught by the Sisters of

Mercy, and never before and never since have I witnessed a name being so completely misrepresented by a few.

When the Sisters of Mercy first arrived in Kilrush on May 1, 1855, their intentions truly were good and merciful. During the Great Irish Famine of 1845-1849, Kilrush and the surrounding West Clare area had suffered more than any other area in Ireland. Its people had witnessed heartrending scenes of men, women and children dying of starvation and fever. The arrival of the battering ram was a familiar sight, as cottiers and tenant farmers were evicted for non-payment of rent to absentee landlords. (The battering ram was a contraption consisting of a heavy pole, often iron-shod, suspended from a kind of tripod and brought to bear with a rush on the doors and walls of a house. Nothing could withstand it.) So the starving masses crowded into Kilrush, in hope of getting into the workhouses, where they would receive some food and a place to stay.

In May 1854, three Jesuit priests conducted the first ever mission in the parish of Kilrush. It lasted for three weeks and was attended by the people of neighbouring parishes as well. It was a celebration of hope and gratitude by a people whose faith had sustained them during the rigours of the Penal Laws and the scourge of the Great Famine.

At the close of the mission, the parish clergy, the Jesuit priests, and the parishioners held a meeting during which it was determined that the people of Kilrush wished to perpetuate the memory of the glorious Jesuit mission. As a lasting commemoration of the event, they decided to establish immediately a branch of the Sisters of Mercy in the town, and they called upon every lover of purity, virtue and religion to assist in this great work.

Immediate steps had to be taken to establish a Convent of Mercy. Funds had to be raised, and a suitable site upon which to build the convent had to be found. A committee of thirty was elected to get the job done. Colonel Crofton Moore Vandeleur, the local landlord, had donated a site for the parish Church in 1839. Hoping that he would be equally generous on this occasion, the committee contacted him in Baden, Germany, by a letter requesting a site for the convent. He refused, saying that "Kilrush did not need nuns except for the honour and glory of it," and this refusal angered the townspeople. Realising that it would be years before a convent would be built, the citizens of Kirush established a temporary residence on Frances Street.

One year later, six Sisters, a novice, and a postulant came to Kilrush. They engaged immediately in the works of mercy, visiting the sick and poor in their homes and teaching in the Girl's National School on Chapel Street (where I lived). The vast majority of the people of Kilrush had never before seen a nun and showed a great interest in the Sisters who walked the streets of town dressed in their religious habits.

In June 1861, Colonel Vandeleur, finally having changed his mind, offered the Sisters their choice of a site for the convent, and the lease included a yearly rent of five shillings for a term of 999 years. The school section was constructed in 1864 and was opened as a school for girls, which quickly filled up. And so the nuns got going on their work proper.

Some years later, it was decided to seek educational facilities for the boys of the town. The parish priest applied to the Superior of the Christian Brothers, who then did come to Kilrush and began teaching on May 1, 1874.

While I was in primary school, the Catholic Church's method of preparing young children to enter society was through the use of corporal punishment. My early dealings with the Sisters of Mercy were not good; in fact, little or no mercy was shown to me. I was often dragged, kicking and screaming to the office of Sr. Bridget, who punished her students for passing notes or talking in class with a thick stick across the palms of their hands. I was declared and found guilty (without a hearing to defend myself), sentenced, and taken to be punished. My experiences in primary school forever soured my opinion of the Sisters of Mercy, even though they were not all mean spirited.

Sr. Bridget played a huge role in making my life miserable during my eight years of incarceration in primary school. There was not much pure or virtuous about her, but she certainly knew how to cram religion down my throat. Wearing the black and white nun's habit, as was customary in those days, she patrolled the corridors watching us with her beady, little eyes that peeked out through the thick lenses of her glasses. She was tall and skinny. Black, short hair stuck out from under her veil, and she was constantly trying to push it back under with one hand, only to have it stick out a few minutes later. I determined that this failure to control her own hair was a great source of frustration for her, and she unconsciously took that frustration out on me. She had a high-pitched voice that made me shudder whenever it was directed toward me, which was all too often. When I was standing before her in her office, she would glance down on me with a disappointed look on her face and give a slight shake of her head.

"What am I going to do with you, Monica?" she would ask. "How many times have you to be told to be quiet in class? I want you to write one hundred times *'I must pay attention in class,'* and hand it in to me tomorrow morning. Do you hear me?" she'd ask.

"Yes, Sister."

I knew what was coming next.

"Put out your hands," she'd demand.

I would put my hands out in front of me with my palms up and, from a three-foot stick she kept behind her desk for such occasions, I'd receive three to six blows—depending on how angry she was—on each hand. Raising her right hand (the one that failed to control her hair) high over her head, she brought the stick down with as much force as she could muster. The stinging blows usually landed across my palms, but occasionally missed and landed across my fingertips instead, which hurt so much more and left them numb for a while. My red and swollen hands were gingerly stuffed into pockets or hidden behind my back as I forlornly made my way to my classroom. When sensation finally returned, my hands would tingle for what seemed like hours. Sitting in my seat, I found myself gazing out the window and wishing I were a bird so I could fly away.

I often had to write one hundred times "I must pay attention in class," or "I will not pass notes again," or—my favourite—"Jesus is watching me," which was Sr. Bridget's attempt at giving me a conscience by reminding me that Jesus knew when I was bad. The day she gave me that one to write, I came up with a plan.

Possessing a rather rebellious spirit, I decided to make an otherwise tiresome task fun and get back at Sr. Bridget at the same time. First I wrote one hundred times on the same page the word "Jesus," and then the word "is" on another page, and then the word "watching," and so forth until I had written each word the demanded number of times but not in sentence form. Usually when the punishment work was handed in the next morning, it was briefly glanced at and then thrown in the rubbish bin. On this occasion, Sr. Bridget decided to inspect my work, and, when she opened the pages, she almost hit the roof.

Turning her head sharply in my direction, she demanded, "What's the meaning of this?"

"Ahhh..." I desperately racked my brain for a good response.

"I have never experienced such insolent and brazen behaviour in all my years as principal. Do you think you're funny?" she shrilled at me.

Her voice always raised a few octaves when she was enraged. I loved to hear it because I knew then that I had really riled her up. Victory was mine, and any punishment she cared to dish out was fine by me. It was worth seeing her eyes bulge, her cheeks get flushed, and her voice go off the scales.

"What did I do wrong?" I asked innocently.

"I told you to write one hundred times 'Jesus is watching me,'" she said.

"I did, Sister. Look: here's *'Jesus'* written one hundred times, and here's *'is'* written one—"

"You cheeky thing," she interrupted. "If you think you're going to get away with this, you have another thing coming. Tonight you will write five hundred times in neat, *complete* sentences 'I will do my punishment without insolence' and have your mother or father sign your work."

"Ah, Sister," I protested, "that will take me all night."

"If it takes you all night, then all the better. You need to learn not to be cheeky with me. Now get over here."

Out came the stick and down came the blows.

"So what did you learn, Monica?" Sr. Bridget quizzed me out of breath.

"That Jesus is watching me," I replied in a demure tone of voice.

"And I think that He is very disappointed in you," she added. "I want you to go to confession this Saturday and confess all your sins to get back in His good graces."

"I'll do that, Sister," I lied.

I often wondered if Jesus was watching Sr. Bridget as well, and why He didn't do something to help me. It felt very lonely standing in front of that nun totally powerless and scared. I learned way back when I was only seven not to cry. I saw the glint of sadistic satisfaction in her eyes the first time my tears began to fall, and I sucked in my breath and willed those tears to stop. From that day on I would glare at her with hatred and anger in my eyes as I boldly faced her tyranny. Someone once told me a little trick to ease the blows of the stick: spitting on my hands before holding them out. The spittle caused the stick to slide slightly across the palms, thus lessening the impact. It was another small way to rebel, and it worked well enough for me.

We had a nun in second class whose weapon was the drumstick. She kept it on her piano, and, whenever students got out of line, that drumstick would land across their backs. This woman was unorganised, and her piano was buried beneath piles of sheet music. Everything was out of order in that classroom; it was easy to lose something in the mess, which is exactly what we did with her drumstick one day. It was a simple plan really, and one that worked so well we were free of the drumstick for a week.

Sr. Immaculata, or Sr. Tomato, as was her nickname, searched high and low for her prop, and she had the whole class looking with her. It amazed us that she actually thought we would give her the drumstick if any one of us found it. Eventually our hiding place was discovered, when she removed a pile of sheet music from the top of her piano. She had been looking for a hymn to teach us for the next Sunday's mass. Now a hymn is a song of praise, but we didn't feel much like praising then. One week without the worry of a drumstick landing across our backs if we said the wrong thing was worth being thankful for, but singing praises to God was too much to ask. If only I had had enough courage to break the bloody thing and throw it out the window! I have dreamed of doing just that many times since.

Caroline Morris was my friend in third class. She was a small, quiet girl with curly dark brown hair and brown eyes. Her family had just moved to Kilrush from Tipperary so Caroline was shy, and I saw it as my job to protect her. When Sr. Vincent yelled at her one afternoon for getting something wrong, poor Caroline just burst into tears. I stood up in class all angry and upset and told Sr. Vincent that she was being mean and to leave Caroline alone.

"Come up to my desk, Monica," Sr. Vincent said.

I did as I was told, got up from my seat and walked tentatively towards her desk.

"Now, Monica, what goes on in my class between me and another girl is none of your business, and I'll ask you to keep your comments to yourself."

"But she's new here and you're embarrassing her," I explained in my best tone of voice. I believed what I was doing was right.

Sr. Vincent understood what I was trying to do. Nevertheless, she was the law, and I had crossed the line. Repeatedly banging the side of my head in the same spot with the pointy top of a biro, she leaned close to my ear and called me a scallywag. That's what she called us when she thought we were being silly. The biro started to really hurt me, and, much to my consternation, I burst out crying.

"Ah, that didn't hurt all that bad, Monica. Go sit down now and stop your crying."

When I got back to my seat, Caroline was still sobbing at the desk next to me with her head on her arms. I joined her and together we cried until the final bell for the day rang and we could go home. I struggled to control my tears and remove all traces of them from my face before I went home. My parents were already trying to change the system and have corporal punishment stopped in our school. Until they succeeded, they asked each of us to cooperate with the nuns and brothers, and to be on our best behaviour. They would not have been angry with me, but they would have been furious with Sr. Vincent, and either my mother or father would have marched up to Sr. Bridget's office and raised holy hell. In the long run, that only came back to make my life more miserable, so I learned not to tell them all that went on at school.

When my sister Mary was in third class, she did something that angered Sr. Vincent, and I witnessed her being dragged by two of her classmates up the corridor to the witch's lair. Sr. Vincent led the procession, and I yelled "traitors" to the two girls who were dragging poor Mary. Just like I had been, she was kicking and screaming and fighting like mad to break free. I empathised with her plight completely.

While in fourth class, I was caught cheating during a test. I was grabbed by my long blond hair and spun around a few times before being released. I went spinning backwards into the blackboard while my chair skidded across the classroom in the opposite direction. Sr. Magdalene was a sweet, kind, and quiet nun most of the time, but she possessed a terrible temper. It is written in the Bible, in the Book of Proverbs, *"Beware the fury of the patient man,"* and it was so true in her case. After leaping from her chair, she would march to the blackboard and rapidly draw two huge circles next to each other. In the first circle she would write in tiny writing the word "me," and in the other circle the same word but, this time, gigantic, taking up the entire circle.

"This is what you're supposed to be like," she would say pointing to the first circle, "a little me in the whole world taking up just a tiny bit of space. But no, you are selfish and inconsiderate, and you want to take up the whole world and not leave room for anyone else." She'd emphasise her point by banging the circle containing the gigantic "ME," with the piece of chalk. I would laugh along with the rest of the class, but inside I'd be hurt and upset, knowing she thought that way of me.

The memory that angers me the most is of the day I walked past Sr. Bridget's office to go home when school was over. It was the September of my final year of primary school; the last year of having to put up with her had just begun. She came running out of her office as I passed and called my name.

"Monica, come here a minute."

"Yes, Sister?" I inquired calmly while I fretted inside over what I could possibly have done wrong now.

"I need you to clean my office for me. There's a good girl," she said.

"But I'm going home," I protested.

"It won't take you long, and I'll give you something when you're done," she promised.

Well, the prospect of a reward always worked for me, so I quickly agreed and went to work cleaning and organising her office. I straightened out all her desk drawers, dusted the blinds and shelves, filed away all the papers on her desk, swept the carpet, and emptied the rubbish bin, which was overflowing with some poor soul's one hundred sentences. It took me over an hour, and the whole time I worked I wondered what reward she would give to me. I hoped it would be money because I was saving for a bicycle of my own, and every penny I earned went into the bank. I thought that a one-pound note would be a fair reward for cleaning her office. When finished, I went to find Sr. Bridget to tell her I was done and to collect my reward. She came back to the office with me to inspect my work and was very impressed with how well I had cleaned. Reaching into the top drawer of her desk, she pulled out a small laminated picture of Jesus.

"You did a great job, Monica. Here you go," and she handed me the picture.

I was speechless and could feel the rage well up inside of me.

"Go on home now and thank you," she said, oblivious to the fact that she had just shattered any remaining good will I may have had toward her.

As I walked down the corridor, I threw the picture of Jesus into the rubbish bin. Why was *He* always thrown in my face? He was used to make me feel guilty; to keep me in line, and then His picture was given to me as a reward. Talk about receiving mixed messages. If it were not for my mother and father teaching me the wonderful person Jesus actually was and of all the good He did for mankind, I would have hated Him and forever associated Him with Sr. Bridget. She used religion as a means of controlling me through fear and guilt, and that was wrong. I knew it then, even as a child. I avoided Sr. Bridget like the plague after that day and was only caught a couple more times and told to clean her office. In my dreams, I had revenge on her, and it felt oh so good.

When I was seventeen, that dream came true. On my very last day of secondary school, when my final exams were completed and I was walking down the hill, I spied Sr. Bridget lying on a towel in the sun, on the playground of the primary school. I made a beeline for her, realising that this was my chance to say to her what I had been unable to put into words when I was younger. Standing directly in the sun's rays and casting a shadow along the length of her body, I waited for her to notice my presence. Her eyes soon opened to see what was blocking the sun, and she sat up when she saw me. Not giving her a chance to say a word, I blasted her with every curse word I could remember. As she sat there with her mouth wide open in shock, I continued to tell her exactly what I thought of her and why. Tears appeared in her eyes, and she apologised profusely, saying that she never realised how I felt, and that she hadn't intended to be so mean. I softened when I saw her tears and began to feel sorry that I came on so strong. She asked for my forgiveness, which I gave to her, but it took me years to actually forgive her completely.

Looking back over my years of primary school as the final bell rang that last day, I could recall many other times when I had been embarrassed, humiliated, frightened, and abused. There had been happy memories, too, but to a sensitive child as I was then, the moments of fear and pain have stayed in the foreground of my mind and will never be forgotten.

As I slowly gathered my books and made my way down the corridor past Sr. Bridget's office and out the door, I turned and looked back one last time at the walls that had held me prisoner against my will. I didn't go crazy like the other children, but my spirit was singing as I walked home to freedom. A bad chapter in my life was over, and new adventures lay ahead; I anticipated going to secondary school in the autumn.

The summer that followed proved to be the best summer of my life. It was 1980, and I was twelve years old. That July I would enter my teenage years. I couldn't wait.

Chapter Two
The Setting

*I yearn, I hope, I wish to be
Back there among my friends,
In Kilrush town in County Clare,
Where flow of Shannon never ends.*

From *Before All of My Living Dies*
Author unknown

Kilrush, or *Cill Rois* in Gaelic, means "the church of the woods." It is a small and busy market town in West Clare, one mile from the River Shannon. Unemployment has always been a problem, so many young people moved to the cities or emigrated to England, America or Australia in order to find work.

Growing up with the people who stayed was a pleasure. Everyone had time to stop and talk to each other. The common greeting was "Well," which was short for "Are you well?" or "Soft day, thank God," which was usually said on days when the rain fell softly and did not pour. In times of trouble, neighbours helped one another by visiting the sick and bringing food and the daily gossip.

My family was not native of Kilrush. My mother hailed from Tuam, a small town in County Galway where I was born, and my father was born in St. Monica's parish, in the Upper West Side of New York City. It was the nature of the people from the West of Ireland to be very clannish. Being a "Yank," it took my father (and the rest of his family by association) years to no longer be considered outsiders. We had no relatives in Kilrush at all, and that alone made us very unique. I believed that was why we were picked on in school.

Kilrush is very old and abounds with history and folklore. I grew up hearing many stories, like the one about the Spanish Armada, which was a fleet of ships sent by Spain to attack England in 1588. A terrible storm arose during the course of the battle. The Spanish ships were defeated, and many of them were blown away to the north, along the east coast of England, north of Scotland. They couldn't get back to Spain through the English Channel from whence they came, so they sailed due west, intending to come down in a southwesterly direction after some time and make for Spain that way. Some turned too soon and wound up in Scotland, and many of them landed in Ireland. Seven ships of the Spanish Armada sailed up the mouth of the River Shannon and anchored just off shore from Kilrush. Six of the seven ships were in good shape while the seventh, the *San Marcos*, was near sinking, and the Spaniards decided to burn her. The Spaniards had run out of water and came to Kilrush offering to exchange a cask of wine for every cask of water they were given. However, a strict command had come from London to say that no one was to give any assistance to the survivors of the Spanish Armada under penalty of death. No matter how hard the Spaniards bargained, they were eventually turned away without any water, and they were forced to pull up anchor and sail elsewhere. Such was the power of England over the kind, generous, and always helpful people of Kilrush.

In 1600, many of the Irish did not want to accept English rule, and a war was conducted against them in order to stamp out their resistance. Sir George Carew was the Queen's Deputy in charge of pursuing and subduing the Irish chieftains in County Kerry, across the river Shannon from Clare. Apparently he had some difficulty marching to Kerry the usual way, which was through Limerick, so he headed for Kilrush instead. Carew quartered his troops of over one thousand foot soldiers and seventy-five horses in town until sufficient boats were found to transport them across the Shannon. Once in Kerry, they took possession of Carrigafoyle Castle, which is west of

Tarbert and can be seen from the Aylevaroo, the beautiful coastline of the Shannon, just south of Kilrush.

While standing at the top of Aylevaroo, you can gaze across the blue waters of the Shannon toward the Slieve Mish mountains behind Tralee, and Mount Brandon in Kerry's Dingle Peninsula, and follow the coastline between the heads of Kerry and Clare to the ever-widening mouth of the river where it enters the Atlantic Ocean. In the foreground, two islands can be seen. The smaller one is called Hog Island and has nothing of interest except twenty acres or so of open green fields. Cows and horses are periodically forced to swim there to graze. Scattery Island is much larger and derived its name from the Old Norse spoken by the Vikings, who established a base on the island in the tenth century. The old Gaelic name for the island is *Inis Cathaigh*, which means "island of battles." In the early part of the sixth century, an Irish saint called Senan established a monastic settlement there. Senan was believed to be either the figurehead of a pagan cult that had been christianised, or the leader of a band of hermits who would not allow women on the island. A 120-foot-high round tower, or *clogas*, that was built by Saint Senan could be seen from miles away. It became the subject of many local stories and poems.

Round tower, symbol of our ancient lore,
Your pinnacle seen from mainland shore,
Still stands steadfast on island base,
About you Shannon waters race.

Your walls were shaped by sweat and prayer,
By monks who toiled with love and care,
Raised stone on stone with purpose clear,
To reach the top, feel Heaven near.

"Round Tower"
Author unknown

The ruins of seven churches, a well, the burial place of Saint Senan, and the remains of an Elizabethan castle are scattered around the island. The remains of a small village can be found to the south of the pier, and a schoolhouse to the north. The last people left the island in October 1978, and the only daily visitor since has been the tide. During the tourist season, boatloads of tourists are brought to the island to explore the ruins, and some local lads row there to do a bit of drinking, away from the watchful eyes of their parents and the *Gardai*. At the southern end of the island, there is a lighthouse that helps to guide ships up the Shannon and keep them away from the rocks.

When I was growing up, the only religion in town was Roman Catholic, but there was a time when that religion struggled to exist. In the early part of the 1600s, the Dutch and English Protestants had been brought to the town by the Earl of Thomond, O'Brien, who had gone over to the English side. These people took over the Catholic Church—the original church in the woods from which Kilrush got its name. Having no place to worship, the parish priest was forced to accept an alternative of two cabins joined together in a place called Ball Alley Lane, which ran from Moore Street to Burton Street, opposite to Stewart Street. This lane was just over the back wall of the garden behind my house. The Catholics worshiped there for about one hundred and fifty years, until a building at the corner of Burton Street and High Street was converted into a church. Mass was offered there until 1839, when Colonel Crofton Vandeleur donated a site for the Catholic Church that is still in use today.

In 1980, Kilrush was the second largest town in Clare with a population of approximately thirty-five hundred people. It was bordered on the east by the Kilrush Wood, on the south by the River Shannon, and on the west and north by rocky farmland and bogs. To a curious and imaginative twelve-year-old girl, it was the perfect backdrop to the theatre of life, which unfolded daily dramas of tragedy, comedy, or the mundane, and provided excellent locations for adventure.

I saw my intrinsic identity to be that of an explorer, and I made it my mission to explore every nook and cranny of my hometown and its surrounding areas. The places mentioned in the history books were in ruins and therefore cloaked in mystery. Ghosts were seen in the bell tower of the Protestant Church; they lurked in the dark and musty cells of the old jail; they still entertained in the Vandeleur house in the Wood; and my father saw one over the range in the kitchen of my house. Each adventure I had was dipped in the past and enriched by folklore and tradition. Many times, being an explorer took a lot of courage.

Thankfully, I was not alone. Being the third child of six children, I never lacked a companion on my various journeys. I have two older sisters, Kathleen and Mary, plus two younger brothers, and a younger sister—Skip (John), Michael and Grace respectively. Michael is the youngest. Together we went through our childhood exploring the surrounding countryside, watching the animals and birds, learning about indigenous plant life, creating imaginary adventures stimulated by the abundant mystery and adventure books that filled our library at home, and generally enjoying the freedom of youth. I could not accept my ascribed position of "female" and always believed I was supposed to be a boy. I struggled to achieve equality with the lads and proved to be a better climber, fighter and runner than many, so I was accepted as one of them.

Music was constantly playing on the stereo at home, ranging from opera, classical, soft rock, jazz, R&B, big band, to children's records. The radio was turned on for the news, Mam's lunchtime soap—"Harbour Hotel"—and other programs of interest. Reading is one of my father's passions, so he encouraged us to read, telling us that books were the greatest educators. Television was not allowed in our home—in fact, we did not own one, so we were forced to use our own imaginations to entertain ourselves. I once read that books were the windows to the imagination. With minds filled with stories of fairy forts and trees reaching up through the clouds to magical lands, pirates, animal hunters, space adventures, cops and robbers, cowboys and Indians, and crime solvers, we never lacked ideas for our own adventures.

Of all my siblings, I got along with Skip the best, and I shared most of my adventures with him. Different children were with us at different times, but we were the main characters in whatever drama was unfolding. Skip was two years younger than I, and he thought himself hot stuff after having turned eleven in May. He was short for his age and somewhat on the skinny side, with light brown hair and soft, gentle blue eyes.

"Want to go up the fields for a scrap?" Skip would ask me on days when there wasn't much to do.

"Okay," I was quick to agree, and we'd cross the street and go up Chapel Drive and into the fields on the other side. A "scrap" was what we called wrestling, and it was our favourite thing to do together. As soon as we got to the middle of the first field, Skip would tackle me and over we'd go, rolling around and having great *craic* until one of us got hurt. Then the fight became a real one, with fists flying and knees jabbing. We'd stop as soon as we both were exhausted, and head for home to fight again another day.

I grew up in a house that was built before the Great Famine of 1845. It is in fact on a map of Kilrush dated 1841. The owner at that time, Jack O'Dea, was a carpenter and an undertaker, and he ran his business out of the front portion of the house. I often thought the ghost my Dad saw over the range was a trapped soul belonging to one of the dead people Mr. O'Dea built a coffin for and laid out in the front room.

At that time, the Vandeleurs were landlords and owned the entire town, and everybody who had property, whether a house or shop, only owned their house or shop and not the ground beneath it. Everyone paid ground rent to the Vandeleurs up until recent times. My parents actually had to buy out our ground rent so that they owned the entire property—house and ground—in what is called "freehold."

The Vandeleur family was the most prominent landlord family in West Clare. They were of Dutch origin, and established the family estate in Sixmilebridge in the 1630s. They prospered after being reimbursed by the Cromwellians for losses during the 1641 rebellion, when the local Irish rose up and took over some of the settlers' property. This property had belonged to the Irish until it was taken from them and given to the settlers. Giles Vandeleur, who was High Sheriff of the county in 1665, purchased a large portion of land in West

Clare from O'Brien, the Earl of Thomond, and this he consigned to his son, the Rev. John Vandeleur. This portion of land included the Kilrush area, and Rev. John became the first Protestant Rector of Kilrush and the first landlord of the Vandeleur family in Kilrush. He was succeeded by his son John in 1727, who was in turn succeeded by his son, Colonel Crofton Vandeleur. Until the succession of Crofton Vandeleur, the family name was a respected one around Kilrush. Despite his role in the famine evictions, scorn and hatred were reserved for Hector Vandeleur, who became landlord in 1881. He was an absentee landlord of the worst kind and only paid one visit to Kilrush to inspect his inheritance in 1882. In October 1887, he started evictions in Kilrush town that continued until the end of July 1888. Due to the Land League and Land Purchase Act, site settlements were eventually reached, and the evicted tenants were allowed back to their holdings. At last the power of the Vandeleurs was broken.

Many of the streets of Kilrush are named after members of the Vandeleur family: Frances, John, Moore, Grace, Henry, Hector, and Vandeleur Streets. Many of their dead are interred in a great tomb in the old Protestant graveyard.

With all of this history and folklore adding fuel to the passionate fire within my soul, I could not wait for school to end. I had been counting the days for weeks now, and Skip and I already had plans made and were ready to go. So when I walked out the doors of primary school and into the sunshine, my mind was on all the places I would explore during the summer. In two weeks I would be getting my own bike, which I had saved a whole year to buy. I would no longer be bound by the distance I could walk in one day, but by how far I could cycle, and that opened up so much more territory for my curious spirit to roam.

Chapter Three
Bonfire Night

Spin earth!
Tumble the shadows into dawn,
The morning out of night;
Spill stars across these skies
And hide them with the suns.
Teach me to turn
My sullen sense toward marvel.

Raymond J. Baughan

June 23rd is St. John's Eve, or Bonfire Night, as it was more often called, and it was my official start to the summer holidays, although school didn't end for another week. I looked forward to it for weeks and eagerly took part in its preparation. Two bonfires were lit to celebrate this Christian/pagan tradition. One was at the far end of town, up on Pella Road by the old dump. The other was on my side of town, at the end of Moore Street where it meets Grace Street and Russell Lane, right outside the old Protestant Church. Where the two streets and the lane came together, there was an open expanse of ground that served as a car park at Christmas time when the only service of the year was held at the church. At that time, the few remaining Protestants who lived in the countryside and the majority of Catholics crammed into the little old church for a non-denominational service to celebrate the birth of Jesus. I remember going one year with my sister Kathleen and sitting way in the back on an old and worn, musty-smelling red velvet-cushioned seat. The whole church smelled like must and mildew, and the atmosphere among the townspeople was one of intrigue and curiosity, to be sitting in a foreign church of a foreign religion. There was respect as well, and a spirit of oneness and acceptance. I thought that if only this feeling could be felt between the Protestants and Catholics in the North, there would be no need for violence. I had a simple solution to the problems in the world—love one another. Jesus knew what he was saying when he gave us the Golden Rule *"Do unto others as you would have others do unto you." "Love your enemies."* He knew that where there was love, hatred could not thrive. Smart man!

The Feast of the Nativity of St. John is set down in the papal calendar for the 24th of June. When Pope Gregory I sent his emissaries over Europe toward the end of the sixth century to gather the pagans into the Roman church's fold, he instructed them to meet the pagans half way. Thus the pagan mid-winter celebration of Yule was consecrated as the birthday of the Saviour and became Christmas, and the pagan mid-summer celebration was adopted as the feast of John the Baptist, who was born six months before Jesus in order to announce his arrival. It was John who baptized Jesus in the River Jordan for which Jesus referred to him as: *"A burning and shining light."* Accordingly the Church could, in good conscience, instruct congregations to light their midsummer fires as they had always done, but to turn their thoughts to St. John instead of the sun. So the holiday continued to flourish across Europe disguised in a threadbare Christian cloak, and it wasn't difficult for the pagans to enter the church's fold.

Every year we built our bonfire to the right of the main gates, which led into the church grounds and the graveyard behind, and far enough away from the stone wall so as not to set the ivy on fire. That had happened the year before when we built the bonfire too close to the wall, and the fire brigade had to be called to put out the blaze. Not only did the firemen put out the fire on top of the wall, they also extinguished our bonfire and hence our fun. The building of a bonfire is not something to be taken lightly, especially when competing with a rival neighbourhood. In order for it to be the biggest, tallest, and smokiest, certain steps had to be taken. The adults and teenagers were in charge of its construction, and all the little children helped to gather the necessary combustible items. St. John's Eve or midsummer's approach was heralded by droves of young children begging combustibles for the community bonfire. We scrounged the town dump, building sites, back yards, and garages for anything that could be burned. People donated broken chairs, wooden bed frames, mattresses, chests of drawers, tables, old clothing, worn rugs and pieces of carpet, and anything else they could think of. Skip and the lads were in charge of getting together as many old and used lorry and car tires as possible, which were piled on top of the bonfire as its crown. One day Skip and his best friend Martin Galvin found two huge used lorry tires up in the old dump. With sticks in hand, they proceeded to attempt to roll the tires across town, down Chapel Street and around the corner to the site of the bonfire. Once the tires built up momentum at the top of Chapel Street, Skip and Martin could be seen running helter-skelter alongside the tires using the sticks to control their direction and speed. These tires were much too big, however, and quickly the situation got out of hand as Skip's tire gathered too much speed and took off with a mind of its own down Chapel Street. Screaming and yelling at the top of his lungs, Skip chased after the runaway tire.

At the bottom of the hill, Moore Street intersects Chapel Street perpendicularly with a row of shops and houses on the other side. Leaving Skip in its dust, the tire managed to cross Moore Street and slam into the wall of Kennedy's shop without hurting anyone. It was a knackered and much-relieved Skip who eventually caught up with the tire and, very carefully this time, guided it to the bonfire.

Bonfires have been lit in Kilrush for hundreds of years and will continue to be lit as long as people are around to light them.
Lady Wilde, the great chronicler of Irish folklore, described the summer solstice as it was in 19th century Ireland in her book *Ancient Legends, Mystic Charms, and Superstitions of Ireland,* 1887. She wrote:

The sacred fire was lighted with great ceremony on Midsummer Eve; and on that night all the people of the adjacent country kept fixed watch on the western promontory of Howth, and the moment the first flash was seen from that spot the fact of ignition was announced with wild cries and cheers repeated from village to village, when all the local fires began to blaze, and Ireland was circled by a cordon of flame.

The Celts reckoned their days from sundown to sundown, so the June 24th festivities actually began on the previous sundown. So it was that as soon as the sun began to set on June 23rd, one of the men lit the bonfire. The flames were greeted with loud cheers, clapping of hands, and piercing whistles. A great crowd of people from the neighbourhood came out to witness the lighting of the bonfire. Mothers admonished their young children to stay clear of the flames, while older children dared each other to get closer and closer. I just jumped up and down in glee, and a surge of pure happiness swept over me. Looking around at the faces of the people next to me, I could see happiness and excitement in their eyes and smiles on their faces, so happy thoughts must have been going through their heads as well. When the tires burned, they produced a thick, acrid smoke that poured up into the sky and spread out like a black cloud obscuring the stars and filling the eyes, throats and noses of those standing around enjoying the blaze. No one minded the smoke, because the thrill of the bonfire far outweighed the annoyance and burning sensation of a breath of acrid air.

The summer solstice is the longest day and shortest night of the year, and Skip and I planned on staying up the entire night with the lads and the older teenagers and adults. After all, I was almost a teenager myself. Old back seats of cars and deck chairs were placed in a semicircle around the fire, but nobody sat on them. When one of us would go over and sit down, we were yelled at to get off. The seats were for the spirits of the dead who might come to share in the celebration. These spirits were given front row seats to honour their visit and keep them happy. It was always considered prudent to keep spirits happy just in case. Respect for the unknown was a healthy thing, and it didn't do to unwittingly upset whatever lurked in the spirit world. So we stayed clear of the seats and sat instead on the curb outside Mrs. Cahill's house, which was the last house on Moore Street. Every year she sat on her front steps and was guaranteed a good view.

The crowd dwindled quickly after midnight, when all the young children were brought home to bed and parents and the elderly followed behind. There was a tangible change in the atmosphere after that. It was now time to have fun. Out of bags or pockets came aerosol cans with perfectly visible warning labels, saying *"COMBUSTIBLE - keep away from fire."* These were our fireworks. One by one, we ran up to the fire and threw in our cans, then made haste back to our seats to witness the explosion. Pops, bangs, and sizzles continued until our arsenal had expired. We elected a sentinel to keep watch up Moore Street, in case the Gardai came out of their barracks to investigate. No one bothered to come, so the fun continued for hours. By now the fire had died down considerably. Most of the adults had returned to their houses, and all of the front row seats intended for the spirits, were occupied by young lovers who were necking and fondling each other much to my and the lads' disgust.

We had plans of our own. Each of us had brought along a potato to bake in the fire. The embers were still quite hot, so we approached the fire gingerly and placed our potato on the outskirts, careful not to scorch our hands. While they cooked, we told ghost stories and played pranks on the young lovers. In the wee hours of the morning, we sat together on the curb and ate our baked potatoes in happy and tired silence. It was the best baked potato I ever tasted. Soon after, we all went home; our summer holidays were about to begin.

Chapter Four
My Own Bike at Last

One day, the year before, I asked my father for a bicycle of my own. We only had one bicycle the six of us had to share. We divided the week up, and each of us got one day to have the bicycle all to ourselves, and on the seventh day the bicycle rested, just like it said to do in the Bible. My day was Tuesday. However, many situations arose where my friend Tara O' Brien asked me to go cycling with her on a day other than Tuesday. Fights broke out among my siblings and me as I desperately tried to make a deal, in order to change my day and be able to go with Tara. Something had to be done about this problem, so I approached my father to see if perhaps I could have my own bike.

Now money didn't grow on trees in my family, as was pointed out to me on many occasions. Being a reasonable man and understanding my dilemma, Dad suggested a deal. He had a similar deal going with Skip.

"If you save up half of the money, then I will match it and you can buy a secondhand bike from Mr. Hanrahan," he said to me.

"Fair enough," said I, while inside I said to myself that it would take me years to save up the thirty pounds I needed.

It took me exactly one year. I babysat every chance I got, did odd jobs around the house for extra pocket money, and organised boxes of old invoices for a local supermarket. When I had my thirty pounds in the bank, true to his word, Dad added his half of the deal, which he said was an early birthday present. I now had enough money to buy a secondhand bike. It was the end of June, which meant I would have my own bike for the whole summer. I was so excited, and off I went to Hanrahan's repair yard to put in my order. I called it a repair yard, but, in fact, it was the front, side and back property around Mr. Hanrahan's house on Grace Street.

I was no stranger to the repair yard. I'd been a tomboy my entire life; the place was my favourite haunt. It appealed strongly to my adventurous, creative, and mechanical self, and I would spend hours sitting on an empty oil barrel, watching Mr. Hanrahan and his sons put together a bicycle, fix an alternator, or strip an old washing machine for the yards of copper wiring in the motor, which could be sold to a scrap dealer for a good price. If I happened to be there when Mr. Hanrahan was in a drunken state, I was given the motor to strip. Returning home on those lucky days, I'd have red, swollen, blistered, and tingling hands, but I would be proud and feel like a "man."

The place was a jungle of twisted metal, entangled pipes, and machinery parts that climbed upward in majestic, somewhat grotesque heaps. Puddles of dark lubricating oil, some still spurting from a capsized whisky bottle, dotted the pavement. Spanners, pliers, nuts and washers, scattered ball bearings, brake cables, and deflated multi-patched inner tubes were strewn in disarray along the walk. I had to side step delicately past the assorted bicycles, cars, and appliances in various forms of disrepair to make my way towards the operating room, which was situated at the far left-hand corner of the yard.

When I entered the yard on the day in question, a pungent, choking stench of diesel hung thickly over an old, dilapidated tractor whose rust-eaten frame leaned sadly against a rotted, stumbling fence. This ancient relic was destined to be the proud donor of engine parts to a seemingly younger model, which stood naked in the chill evening breeze. Its metal clothing lay in a pile on the ground as the surgeon worked steadily to give it new life.

Mr. Hanrahan wore dirty, grease-stained overalls and brown Doc Martin boots, which had seen better days. His equally dirty, greasy cap sat lopsided on thinning, wiry grey hair. In this ensemble and with a cigarette butt hanging out the side of his mouth, Mr. Hanrahan—even with his twinkling blue eyes and kind smile—didn't portray the image of the brilliant surgeon he was. I had witnessed him jumpstart the engine of an old wreck of a car, which had died peacefully in her sleep, and give to her another few months or years of life in which to provide transportation to her very needy owner. When patients were brought in with dimming or extinguished eyesight, he helped them see again. When they became senile, forgetting to brake, he gave them a drink of brake fluid and the problem was solved. When collision scars ran the length of a patient's body, or corrosion left pox marks on the surface, he performed plastic surgery and sent them home with a whole new image and a fresh coat of paint. I admired, respected and revered the man, and I knew that with his skill he would make for me the best bike in the whole world.

I waited patiently for a break in concentration, and the surgeon finally leaned back for a moment to stretch his aching muscles.

"Excuse me, Mr. Hanrahan, but can I have a minute of your time?" I quickly interjected.

"What's that? Who's there?" he said as he whirled about. "Ah, 'tis you girl and what do you want?"

"I'm here to place an order for a bike," I replied proudly.

"A bike is it then, and how much money do you have?" came the reply from under the bonnet of the tractor. There followed a string of curse words I wasn't supposed to know, but of course I knew them all, and then a spanner was sent flying across the yard. When things didn't go well, Mr. Hanrahan displayed a wicked temper, which sometimes sent me running for my life. This outburst was short-lived, however, and he was soon back under the bonnet whistling tunelessly between his teeth.

"How much would you charge for a secondhand bike?" I asked.

I was not about to tell him how much money I had saved up because that would be the exact price he would charge me. I may have been young but I was no fool, and I had an idea how these sorts of things worked.

"Well, now, that would depend on the type of bike you choose, girl. If you tell me how much you have, then I'll be able to tell you what I can do for you."

"How 'bout I pick out one of the bikes you have lying around over there by the bunker, and then you tell me how much it will cost to have you fix it up and get it looking like new?"

Oh, I'd make a good solicitor one day. I had a natural gift for arguing, as my mother often told me. She also told me I had a natural gift of the gab, which meant I talked a lot. Well, I was in the middle of six children, so how else was I going to be heard?

"Grand job," said the surgeon, and he went back to his operation.

Galvanized iron was stacked against the huge red bunker that held all the useless odds and ends destined for the scrap yard. Weeds and grass had taken root inside tires laying haphazardly in every direction. Tufts of grass also appeared on the roof of the kennel that housed a flea-ridden mutt, who posed as guard dog at night and aggravator during the day.

I had to make my way past the dog to get to the bicycles next to the bunker. I was not generally afraid of dogs, but this mutt was mean. As soon as I took one step in his direction he began to bark and snarl and desperately tried to break the chain that bound him, so he could leap for my throat. Thankfully, the chain was short, and I was able to stay just far enough away so that no matter how hard he tried, he was unable to reach me. Walking in a circle around the kennel and its occupant, I eventually made my way to the bicycles and spent a couple of hours sorting through the mess looking for a frame in good shape and big enough to fit my size. Next, I found two wheels with the same dimensions and a handlebar. All the other parts, such as the brakes, pedals, tires and inner tubes, chain and seat, would be new. I wanted a blue bike with *"Lightening"* written along the frame in silver paint. I would have to do that myself. All I was guaranteed was a sound bike in good working order; how it looked cosmetically was up to me.

When I was finished sorting through the mess and had the parts I needed, I brought everything back to the operating room and lay them down next to the almost finished tractor. Mr. Hanrahan took a look at my collection, asked me what kind of seat and pedals I wanted, then gave me his price.

"That'll cost you fifty quid," said the surgeon, "and I'll have the bike ready for you by the end of next week."

"Grand job," said I, mimicking what he had said earlier.

A spit shake was done, and the deal was set. Now usually I find the idea of a spit shake quite revolting, but when Mr. Hanrahan spits in his hand and extends it in your direction, and you are in desperate need of a bike of your own, then certain otherwise disgusting customs become worth it. So I spat on my hand and placed it in his. The deal was set as if we had signed a contract in front of a solicitor and witnesses. Such was the power of a spit shake in a small town where your word means everything.

I lingered for a little while longer, watching him bring the tractor back to life. Dirt and grease accumulated on everything and tainted objects a dull-grey or soot-black depending on how long they sat there. It stained clothes and skin, stuck to hair, and left me smelling like an old, oily rag.

Totally unorganised, filthy, foul-smelling and noisy were the characteristics that enhanced the air of adventure and mystery that drew me to the yard on many an occasion. The novelty wore off as I outgrew my tomboy years and became a young lady, but I still look back on those days and remember Hanrahan's repair yard, and especially the summer when I got my first bike.

Lightening and I had many a grand adventure that summer and for years to follow. She served me well, and we were the best of friends. I rode her proudly around the town showing off to all who cared to look. I owned my own bike that I had worked hard for a year to buy, and nothing could stop me now. Tuesdays and all the other days of the week, even Sundays, were mine to enjoy.

Chapter Five
A Cycle to Ballybunnion

Hear my brother singing
Sweetly in the night,
Sweetly softly singing
Songs of fierce delight.

Simple songs of wild joy,
Piercing my spirit,
Fill the night with music
For those who hear it.

From *Brother Curlew*
by John P. McCormack

    Around the time I got my bike, Skip also got his bike. He painted his orange, and in black paint along the cross bar, the words *"The Flying Dutchman."* Our excitement was so intense that we were like two little children on Christmas morning. Lightening and The Flying Dutchman were ready for their first adventure, and we didn't want to disappoint them. We wanted their first adventure together to be an unforgettable one, so cycling the five miles around the Aylevaroo or eight miles to Kilkee just wouldn't do.
    "How 'bout we go all the way to Ballybunnion?" Skip suggested.
    "Jaysus, Skip, that's maybe fifty miles away," said I, amazed that he thought we'd be able to cycle that far in one day.
    "Nah, it's more like twenty," said Skip. "Let's check with Dad."
    So we asked Dad. Now you never got a straight answer from our

father. Instead of just telling you what you wanted to know, he would take you over to his floor-to-ceiling bookcases in the living room and show you where the reference books or maps were, and tell you to look it up yourself. That's what he did with us this time, too. We got out the map of Western Ireland and found Kilrush in County Clare and Ballybunnion in County Kerry. Ballybunnion is a lovely seaside resort town on the western shore of Kerry. It has sandy beaches, grand big cliffs, amusement parks with bumper cars and slot machines, and brilliant playgrounds. Mam had taken us there a couple of times the summer before by bus, and we had a fantastic time altogether.

Following the scale on the bottom of the map, we were able to measure the distance between the two towns and then calculate how many miles away from each other they were. It was five miles from Kilrush to Kilimer, where the car ferry we had to take across the Shannon River was; then twelve miles from Tarbert, on the other side of the River, to Ballybunnion. All in all, it was a seventeen-mile cycle along heavily travelled main roads. Dad threw a spanner in our plans by telling us we weren't allowed to cycle that far without someone older going with us.

The only person we could think of was Kathleen. She would be turning fifteen that August and was the most responsible and sensible one of the bunch. Also, she had already cycled to many far away places with her friends for weekends and had stayed in youth hostels. We thought that was pure brill'. Skip and I both really admired our older sister. Standing almost as tall as Mam and with long, straight, dark brown hair and bright blue intelligent eyes, she spoke in a soft voice and rarely lost her temper. She was brilliant at everything she did but never got a big head. Anytime we needed help, she was ready to give it to us, and she had the patience of a saint. I knew that from watching her trying to help Skip with his math one night after supper. I would have brained him long ago for being so thick, but she kept at him until he eventually got it.

That night, when Kathleen returned home after working in Coffey's Fish & Chip shop, we begged her to take us for a cycle to Ballybunnion. We must have been very persuasive, because it didn't take her long to agree. Mary heard us trying to bribe her with a free ice cream cone, and a go on the bumper cars, and she became interested as well.

"I want to come too," she said to us.

"All right," Skip and I both answered at the same time. Mary would be turning fourteen in August, and if she were coming too, Dad would definitely say okay.

"It would be best to go one day during next week when I'm not working, then the roads might not be so busy with cars going to the beach." Kathleen said.

"What day are you off?" I asked.

"Tuesday," she answered.

Tuesday was my luck day!

So, we set about making all the necessary plans. Kathleen found out what the schedule was like on Tuesday for the car ferry. From April to September it departed from Kilimer every hour on the hour with the first sailing at 7:00 a.m. and the last sailing at 9:00 p.m. From Tarbert, it departed on the half-hour from 7:30 in the morning until 9:30 at night. Two ferries made the crossing every day. The *Shannon Heather* was built in 1968 and was capable of holding thirty cars. Her sister, the *Shannon Willow*, was brand new and only running one year. She could hold forty-four cars. They were both owned and operated by a private company called Shannon Ferry Limited. We knew the men who collected money for the tickets and hoped we would be allowed to cross for free. It only cost fifty pence for a bike to cross, but that was the price of one go on the bumper cars and we preferred to save our money for that.

The Kilimer-to-Tarbert car ferry helped to forge a great social, commercial, and tourist link between Clare and Kerry, and it united the major tourist areas of Clare, Galway, and Connemara in the north with the Ring of Kerry, Killarney, and West Cork in the south. The Shannon River separated these two areas until May 29, 1969, when the car ferry was officially opened. Droves of romantics were drawn across on the ferry each year for the Rose of Tralee festival in Kerry and the Lisdoonvarna festival in North Clare. Entire circuses have been transported across the river, and lorries of all kinds used the ferry daily for commercial reasons. We wanted to ride on the newer ferry, the *Shannon Willow*, and we looked forward to going up on deck during the twenty minutes it took to cross, to admire the river scenery and see if we could spot any dolphins or porpoises swimming alongside the bow.

Dad made sure that, before cycling any great distance from our house, each one of us could change a flat tire, tighten wheels and handle bars, and fix brakes. We had to check that all the necessary tools, patches and glue were in a little pouch attached to the back of our saddles. We each had to have a bicycle pump clipped to the cross bar, and we were able to carry a small bag with a jacket, beachrobe and swimsuit, lunch, drink, and treats inside, on the carrier over the back wheel. Dad checked each bike to see that it was properly outfitted. Kathleen was to cycle Dad's own bike, which she had taken on her other cycles. Mary had the blue bike we all had shared until recently, and Skip and myself had our very own new bikes.

Early on Tuesday morning, Mam got up and made us a lovely breakfast of creamy porridge, toast, and hot tea. Our goal was to be on the 8:00 a.m. ferry, which meant that we had to leave our house by 7:00 a.m. for the five-mile cycle to Kilimer. As we were heading out the front door with our bikes, Mam stopped Kathleen and gave her a ten-pound note, telling her to treat us to ice cream and some rides in the amusement park. Our eyes lit up in excitement. With ten extra pounds on top of what we each had taken out of our piggy banks, we would be able to go on gangs of rides and even play the slot machines. We gave Mam a great big hug and told her thanks a million, and off we went.

The first leg of our journey, all the way to Kilimer, was mostly uphill. We were excited and full of energy, chatting happily amongst ourselves as we pedaled vigorously. We kept in single file along the main road, with Kathleen in the lead and descending in age order to Skip at the rear. It was a gorgeous day. Not a cloud could be seen in the sky, and the birds sang cheerfully from the Horse Chestnut, Pine, and Sycamore trees that grew right up to the grey stone wall lining the road by the edge of the Wood. The Wood stretched for two or three miles on our left, and open farmland lay on our right. Gorse bushes with their beautiful, small, fragrant yellow flowers filled the air with a sweet smell. At night, high over the fields and Wood, the curlew could be heard tearing the night apart with its sweet, soft song. Early in the morning, the lark greeted the new day with his song as he soared toward the heavens. We heard him singing as we cycled, and we saw swallows darting to and fro and a lone puffin making his way back to the sea.

The road was quiet that early in the morning; the only traffic was the occasional farmer bringing his fresh milk to the creamery and a car or two bringing occupants to work. Some buses and cars passed us going in the same direction, on their way to the ferry no doubt. We made great time to Kilimer and were early for the 8:00 a.m. ferry. We used the loo in the pub at the top of the car park and then went down to the river's edge to wait for the ferry, which we could see approaching slowly from the far bank. A line of cars and tourist buses was gradually forming in the car park, and people were milling about in the early morning sunshine, talking to each other and smiling. As the ferry pulled into the slip, they got back into their respective vehicles and waited for the cars on board to disembark. Then the line disappeared onto the ferry. We were the last ones to board, and after we walked our bikes on deck, the ramp lifted up and the ferry began its crossing.

We had a plan to avoid paying the fifty pence each to cross. As soon as we got on the ferry, we walked our bikes over to where the toilets were, and leaning them against the wall, we ran inside to hide from the ticket man. We watched him go from car to car collecting money for tickets and when he went back into the wheelhouse, we slipped out and mingled with the crowd already dispersing along the upper deck. We were on the newer ferry, *Shannon Willow*, which was painted a brilliant white, with the deck and railings a bright green. Everything was gleaming metal except for the wooden benches on the upper deck, where you could sit and enjoy the ride. We were too excited to sit, and instead ran back and forth and up and down the stairs exploring every nook and cranny of the boat. Skip and I found an excellent spot at the front of the ferry on the upper deck. Leaning over the railing, we could look down on the river, as it seemed to rush by.

"Look, Monica, I see a fin," yelled Skip excitedly.

"Yeah, I see another one over there," I replied, just as excited.

With that, two porpoises leaped in unison out of the water before our very eyes. We were thrilled beyond belief.

"Mary, Kathleen, come over here and see this," Skip yelled.

They came up behind us and watched the porpoises jumping and playing in the river. It looked like they were trying to race the ferryboat. They'd win, no problem, because the ferry wasn't going that fast at all.

All too soon, the shore of Kerry approached and we could see the slip where the ferry docked. A line of cars, buses and lorries were patiently waiting on the other side. We ran to our bikes and walked them to the ramp gate, then waited for the ramp to be lowered and the gate to be opened. We wanted to be the first to get off, just in case the ticket man caught up with us. We were too close now to get stopped and have to pay. Everything worked out perfectly, and before we knew it we were off cycling again towards our destination. This was all new territory for me (other than what I'd seen from the window of a bus), and I soaked it all in as I pedaled my bike. It was a mile cycle from where the ferry docked along the shore of the Shannon to the little town of Tarbert. The tide was way out, and gulls sunned themselves on the exposed seaweed-covered rocks. The air smelled of salt, seaweed, and wet sand. The road curved around to the left. We passed a bar on the right called the Shannon Inn, which was crowded—even this early in the morning—with people waiting for the ferry. We rode along in silence until we got to the town, and then we stopped for a drink from our water bottles and sat on the steps at the base of a stone cross in the middle of the square.

Tarbert was much smaller than Kilrush. It had a small central square and, branching off in the four main directions, were four streets, all lined with brightly painted houses and shops. A housing estate could be seen on a hill along the road we had just taken from the ferry. No one was about. Nothing was open yet, and the cars and buses from the ferry had already passed through ahead of us. So we sat in the warm morning sun and figured out which of the four roads took us to Ballybunnion.

Mary was in charge of the map. She was the leader of the McCormack Gang. Even though Kathleen was the oldest, she didn't come along with us on many of our adventures. She was busy with her own friends. Mary and I didn't always see eye to eye. In fact, if the truth be told, we fought most of the time. We are both Leos and have the natural tendency to lead, and we were stubborn as mules. This combination didn't bode well for harmony in the ranks. However, she was eleven months older than I. Therefore, the title of leader was given to her by virtue of her birth. Mary, with her short dark hair and sparkly blue eyes, was a good three inches taller than I and could beat me in a scrap if she were mad. When we fought, there were no holds barred. Teeth, fists, knees, pinching, head butting, slamming heads against walls, throwing scissors, and pulling hair were all tactics we used in our warfare. Many times we had come away from a fight bloodied and sore, sworn enemies forever, only to be reunited again soon after, when the old jail needed to be explored or the old West Clare Railway beckoned us to follow the ghost tracks once again to Brew's Bridge. Mary fancied herself a keen navigator and was the one who held the compass that indicated where north was when we were exploring new territory. It was only fitting that, on this day, she would be in charge of the map, and I wasn't inclined to fight her for the honour.

As we sipped from our water bottles, Mary spread the map out on the steps. We could see the street sign pointing to Ballybunnion and double-checked its accuracy on the map, just in case some drunken fool had turned the sign around as a cruel joke to tourists. Everything was in order, and it was a straight run the rest of the way to our destination. It was now nine o'clock, and we estimated that we would be on the beach relaxing or jumping in the waves by eleven at the latest.

R551 is the main road from Tarbert to Ballybunnion. It is not a dual carriageway like the one going from Ennis to Limerick, but rather a two-lane local road passing through small villages along the way. The first village we came to was Ballylongford and the next was Astee. I had been told the story that the fabled American outlaw Jesse James hailed from Astee, but I think that was just a local rumour. It was a small little village and, even on bikes, we sailed through it in no time flat. Next stop… Ballybunnion!

Small terraced houses began to line either side of the road as we entered the outskirts of Ballybunnion. The road dipped downhill, and we built up speed as we coursed into the heart of town. We could smell the salt air and hear the waves pounding on the beach to our right, and so we turned in that direction and made our way, using our senses to guide us to the car park at the top of the cliffs. Lining the footpaths were gangs of shops selling all kinds of beach accessories, such as sunglasses, beach chairs, towels, shovels and pails, tanning lotion, umbrellas, kites, beach balls, postcards and T-shirts. We found a place to secure our bikes, and, taking our bags and jackets with us, we headed for the steep steps leading down to the beach.

We swam and jumped in the waves, climbed as high as we dared up the rocky face of the cliff, dug huge holes in the sand, and built a fort with a complicated network of roads, bridges and tunnels leading in and out of our fortress, and when we became hungry, we ate a picnic lunch on our beach robes. After lunch, we decided to make our way up the main street to where we remembered an amusement park to be, from the time we had been there with Mam the year before. The amusement park consisted of an indoor bumper car area and, next to the bumper cars, a great big arcade filled with slot machines and video games. It was noisy and colourful with bright flashing lights and laughing people of all sizes. Mam had hit the jackpot here, and I had stood beside her in utter amazement as hundreds of coins poured out of the machine into her waiting arms, then overflowed onto the floor, rolling about in all directions. I thought that there would be a mad dash to the floor by all the spectators, but no one moved as Mam yelled out "They're mine!" at the top of her lungs. I, of course, had to help her pick up all the money and put it in her handbag, in every pocket of her coat, and some in my own pockets. Mam was tickled pink and proceeded to try every other slot machine in the place, hoping to once again feel the exhilaration of hitting the jackpot. She broke even at the end of the day. I'll never forget the look of bright-eyed excitement I saw on her face that day. She had the time of her life.

I wasn't about to gamble all of my hard-earned money on slot machines. I didn't mind losing a little in the hopes of repeating Mam's lucky pull of the lever, but I had set a limit of one pound for myself, and as soon as I lost that amount, I stopped and moved on to the video games. At least with a video game you got to play a game for a few minutes before your money was gone forever.

The best part of the day for me was when we all went on the bumper cars. We took different cars and proceeded to try to crash into each other as many times as possible before time ran out. On weekdays there were no queues, so we were able to ride the same cars until we ran out of money. We held some money back to buy "99" ice cream cones (soft vanilla ice cream with a chocolate flake stuck in the top), a can of Cidona, and a bag each of periwinkles, which are sea snails, from a vendor in the car park where we parked our bikes. Skip and I had earned money the summer before, gathering periwinkles from the rocks at Cappa when the tide went out and selling them to a man down Pella Road, who, in turn, sold them as a vendor in Kilkee. We had learned how to tell the poisonous horse winkles from the non-poisonous—and rather delicious—periwinkles, and we were very careful not to make a mistake. Can you imagine if someone died from eating a horse winkle we had picked by accident? That would have been terrible indeed!

With our bags of periwinkles, pins to get the sea snails out of their shells, Cidona cans, and ice cream cones in our hands, we found a low wall to sit down upon and enjoy our feast. The sun was long gone behind grey clouds threatening rain at any minute, and we had decided to leave as soon as our feast was consumed. It was half past six, so we had three hours to make the last ferry home at half past nine. We were going to shoot for the half past eight ferry. Dad had warned us not to wait for the last ferry just in case something happened and we missed it. Then we'd be up the creek without a paddle, because the only other way home would be to cycle all the way around to Limerick and then the sixty miles home from there, a total of well over one hundred miles and completely out of the question.

Eating periwinkles is an art and one that I prided myself on having nearly mastered. With the sea snail shell in one hand and the pin in the other, I deftly flicked away the small protective round seal at the opening of the shell with the tip of the pin, and then dipped the pin into the shell to pull out the little snail. The snail held on for dear life, and it took a master to be able to pull out an entire snail and not half of him. I wasn't yet a master, but I was able to pull out a whole snail about three quarters of the time. Periwinkles taste very salty and slightly crunchy around the head area, and delicious going down. I flicked and dipped away, while balancing my ice cream cone between my knees and taking a lick once in a while. There was no fear of the ice cream melting because the air had gotten chilly and damp. We were thankful for our jackets. We continued with our little ritual until all the snails were ingested, the cans of Cidona drained, and the ice cream cones having followed close behind.

With bellies and hearts full of the joys and pleasures of the day, we unlocked our bikes and hopped upon the saddles to begin our return journey. As we laboured up the hill out of town, the sky opened up, and rain lashed against our faces and drenched our trousers below our jackets. From my past experiences, the return journey is usually quicker because it lacks all of the anticipation and excitement that can make the beginning of a journey seem to take forever. All that aside, I had a feeling that this time it would be the return journey that would take forever. Luckily we had given ourselves just under three hours to reach the ferry.

The weather continued to impede our progress. The wind picked up and was blowing against us, which made us have to pedal twice as hard, and the driving rain made it difficult to see very far ahead of us. Buses, lorries, and cars travelling on the road splashed us from head to toe with muddy water. Between Astee and Ballylongford, the weather eased up a bit as the wind died down and the rain turned to

GOODBYE, MY IRISH CHILD

a soft rain and then a fine mist. We were able to take a short break by the side of the road, so we sat on top of a gate going into a field filled with cows, which huddled together for some protection from the rain and a little body warmth. It was a quarter to eight and we still had more than half the way to go. Kathleen said we were better off to keep cycling because at least we were warmer while we pedaled, so off we went again.

About three miles after we passed through Ballylongford, Kathleen got a flat tire, and we had to pull off the road while she fixed it. We were tired and thirsty at this stage, and Skip and I spied a farmhouse a way down a winding wee road off the main one, and we decided to go ask for something to drink. Mary elected to stay behind with Kathleen and keep her company. It was a longer walk than we first anticipated, and when we got to the house, Skip knocked on the front door. It was opened within seconds by a very nice, soft-spoken older woman.

"Do you think we could have some water to drink, please?" Skip asked her.

"We've just spent the day at Ballybunnion," I added, "and we're on our way home when our sister got a flat tire down on the main road."

"Where do ye live?" the woman inquired.

"In Kilrush across the ferry," I answered.

"All the way in Clare!" she exclaimed with surprise on her face. "Ye'er a long way from home love, and it'll be dark soon what with this terrible weather coming our way. Come inside and get warm," she invited.

"We can't stay," said Skip.

"Oh that's right," the woman nodded her head. "Sure, didn't ye leave ye'er sister all alone on the road."

"Nah," said I, "our other sister stayed with her."

"Wait here then, and I'll see what I can give ye," the woman responded and turned and went inside the house. She was back in no time at all with a paper bag filled with ginger snap biscuits and an empty milk bottle filled with orange drink.

"I hope that tides ye over 'till ye get home. May God go with ye," she said, and she made the sign of the cross in our direction as we thanked her and returned to the main road.

Kathleen was furious that we took so bloody long but accepted a couple of biscuits and a swig from the milk bottle nonetheless. Much time had been wasted, and we had our work cut out for us if we were to make the last ferry. We were all quite anxious and afraid of what might happen if we missed it. So, in total silence we pedaled furiously as the last of the sun was swallowed up by the approaching storm.

As we rounded the corner from Tarbert and had the last mile before us yet to cycle, we could see the ferryboat at the slip, and a few cars and buses beginning to board her. We were all quite knackered at this stage but found a reserve of energy deep within ourselves and began to cycle like the wind. When we passed the Shannon Inn, we noticed the ferry begin to pull away from the shore, and we yelled and screamed for it to wait. It seemed like our luck had run out, when all of a sudden the ferry began to back up to the slip. The man in the wheelhouse happened to glance in our direction and noticed four children cycling as fast as we could, and he decided to go back for us. He knew full well the alternative if he left us on the shore. We were so happy to stumble onto the ferry and even happier when the ticket man didn't bother to come and collect our fare; we were totally out of money. As the ferry slowly crossed the Shannon, we huddled in the little waiting room, which was warm and dry and never even bothered to look out the window. Thank God the cycle from Kilimer to Kilrush was mostly downhill because the rain and wind picked up again, and this time is was almost dark. On a clear night, it stays light until eleven during the summer, but in bad weather it gets darker earlier. We reached our front door at just about half past ten, and after putting our bikes in the front hall, we opened the door to the living room and entered the warmth of home at last.

Lightening and The Flying Dutchman had a fabulous first adventure together. They had braved the elements and returned their riders home safely. What more could you ask from a bike?

Chapter Six
The Graveyard Dare

I had always considered myself a brave person afraid of nothing, until one night in early July when something happened to change my mind. Superstitious tales circulated among the older members of our community and were passed down from generation to generation. Tales were told at night by the fireside of ghosts like the Headless Horseman, banshees and wicked fairies that lurked in the spirit world, coming out only at night to work their evil on careless victims. Parents warned of the bogyman that came through bedroom windows at night to carry off bad children. Such nonsense made Skip and me laugh. We weren't afraid until dared by our friends one evening to cross the graveyard that night.

We gathered by the wall across the street from my house that fateful day. I sat on the electric meter box while the lads perched on top of the wall or sat on their bikes with one foot on the ground for balance, leaning over the handlebars and staring at the footpath. It was just far enough into the summer holidays that the novelty of no school had worn off, and we were beginning to be bored with all the free time on our hands.

"Mr. Crowley saw the Headless Horseman come down his lane the other night," said Martin Galvin.

"Go 'way," replied Skip, "he only said that to scare you away from swinging on his gate."

"I wasn't swinging on his gate at all," insisted Martin. "I was just taking a walk for myself down the lane by the river, and he saw me coming. He came out and told me the story. He said that if the Headless Horseman caught any of us alone, he would cut our throats and try to chop off our heads like was done to him long ago. He scared the shit out of me, and I'm never going down there again by myself."

"That's what he was after, you eejit," said I. "He wanted to scare the shit out of you so that you won't swing on his gate while he's away and then leave it open."

Crowley's gate was at the end of the lane going into the woods. It was a big sturdy green wooden gate that ran the width of the lane that became the entrance to Crowley's property. On the other side was an open field where cattle grazed, and beyond the field the woods began and stretched for miles to the south and east. The gate could hold five of us at a time while the others pushed, and we had great craic all together, swinging back and forth across the lane. The goal was to push the gate as hard as possible so that it banged against the wall and knocked off as many gate riders as possible. The gate riders tried to hold on for dear life.

I loved being a gate rider. Stepping onto the bottom rung of the gate and wrapping both of my arms around the top, I would close my eyes and yell "READY." Someone would push the gate with all of the strength they possessed and away I would go, sailing through space and time, waiting with anticipation for the sudden jolt as the gate hit the wall. I prided myself in the fact that I rarely fell off. I so loved the tingly sensation in my tummy and the light-headed feeling as I moved through space. The feeling wasn't there when my eyes were open, and it increased in intensity the more consecutive times I rode the gate. I was good at holding on because if I fell off, I had to push the gate, but if I stayed on, I could ride forever. I quickly became a professional gate rider, much to the annoyance of the lads.

"Ah, Monica, you've been on the gate for ages. Give us a turn," they protested on many an occasion, and reluctantly I would relinquish my turn to let someone else ride.

We held competitions and picked teams and even challenged other children in town. We drove poor Mr. Crowley demented, and he would come charging out of his little house with a pitch fork in his hand and chase us away. That was the highlight of our fun. We would run away as quick as lightening, laughing and cheering and sticking our tongues out. Often enough, we didn't encounter Mr. Crowley at all, and after having our fun swinging on the gate, we just left it open and walked home for our supper. We didn't intentionally leave the gate open, but rather never thought to close it behind us. It was on those occasions that the cows escaped for Mr. Crowley to later find grazing on the grass that grew along both sides of the lane. He had to round them up himself, then drive them back through the gate and into the field where they belonged. I'm sure he had a few choice curse words for us on times like that.

While we were on the subject of the Headless Horseman, Jackie Delaney began telling us a story of the banshee that could be heard wailing in the graveyard at night.

"Me mam told me that it was said to be the ghost of a mother looking for her lost child, and if ever she came across some children out and about instead of being home with their own mother, she would take them away with her," Jackie said.

The others nodded their heads because the same story had been told to them many a time. Skip and I just shook ours and called them all eejits for believing in such rubbish.

"Ok then," said Mickey-Jo Delaney, defending his sister, "If ye are so brave and don't believe these stories, I dare ye to cross the graveyard at midnight tonight. We'll see then who comes back alive or is never heard from again."

The others all agreed with vigorous nods, and their eyes lit up with excitement. At last something interesting was going to happen on an otherwise boring day.

"I dare ye too," said Seamus Flynn.

"Me too," chimed in Brendan and Tara O' Brien in unison.

What could we do? To turn down a dare was equivalent to admitting we liked to watch Sesame Street on the telly. Although we did not own one, we knew all the programs that were okay to watch and those that weren't. After spending years proving that we were tough and brave to the lads and to ourselves, our reputations could now be destroyed. So we accepted the challenge and hoped that no one would show up at midnight to watch.

"Supper's ready. Come and wash up," my mother yelled, as she poked her head out the front door of our house.

"See ye later if ye don't chicken out," said Mickey-Jo Delaney.

"Better bring a flashlight," suggested Tara O' Brien. "It'll be pitch black in there for sure."

"What else should we bring?" I asked, somewhat concerned.

"Well, how about a big carving knife to cut the heads off the bodies when they come out of the graves to get ye?" said Martin Galvin. Martin was tall for his age with wavy blonde hair, blue eyes and a mischievous smile. He lived in the County Council housing estate, Chapel Drive, across from Chapel Street where Seamus Flynn, Jackie and Mickey-Jo Delaney, Tara and Brendan O' Brien lived as well. He had just watched the film *Night of the Living Dead* and couldn't get it out of his mind. That's why my parents wouldn't let us get a telly.

"It's nothing but rubbish and will rot ye'er minds," my father often told us.

"You're not any help at all," I said to Martin, and I headed inside for my supper. If the truth be told, I had completely lost my appetite, and butterflies were beginning to have a field day inside my tummy. Glancing out of the corner of my eye towards Skip as we walked into our house, I could see that he looked a little paler as well. I hoped that he would chicken-out first, and then we wouldn't have to go and I could blame it on him.

Mam had cooked my favourite dinner—steak and corn—and as much as I loved it, on that night I couldn't eat a bite. Skip's dinner was untouched also, and Mam was not happy with us.

"If ye don't finish ye'er supper," she told us, "then ye can go straight to bed after you do the washing up, Monica."

It was my night to do the washing up. Every night the six of us took turns clearing the table and washing the dishes. There was usually a debate after supper as to whose turn it was that night. Mam never forgot and was quick to let the unlucky person know that it was his or her turn. Skip offered to help me out, and together we set about clearing off the dirty dishes and putting them in the basin of hot soapy water. While I washed the dishes, he cleaned the table and the countertop and hoovered the carpet tiles under the table. He left the greasy top of the cooker for me to scrub with Ajax. As we worked, we talked about what was weighing heavy on our minds: the dare.

"Do you still want to go through with it?" asked Skip.

"We have to or we'll be the laughing stock of the town," I answered.

"Maybe there's a way out of this," he said, hopeful that I would have a suggestion as to how we could avoid doing the dare. I didn't.

"Let's face it, Skip. We're stuck, and the only way out is to do it and be done with it," I stated matter-of-factly. "Now in order to stay alive, we're going to have to stay together."

"I thought that you didn't believe in all that rubbish," said Skip.

"I don't, but just in case," I answered. "Tara said that it will be pitch dark in there and she's right, so we had better make sure that our flashlights have good batteries. Mam will kill us if we take her good carving knife, so we'll just have to make do with our penknives. Do you still have yours?" I asked.

"Yeah, it's on my chest of drawers upstairs," Skip replied. "Should we bring some rope, too?" he asked.

"What for?"

"Well, what if we're captured?"

"Oh, and then they can use our rope to tie us both up," I jeered sarcastically.

"No, you fuckin' eejit," said Skip in anger. "So we can get over the wall faster and easier if we have to escape."

"Ah, nothing's going to happen to us," I said. "We'll be in and out before we're even missed. The lads will be more scared than we are, while they're waiting over the wall and not knowing what's going on. That's if they even show up at all."

We really hoped that no one would show up.

After the dishes were done and the kitchen was cleaned, we went upstairs to Skip and Michael's room. We didn't tell any of our other siblings about the dare, in case one of them let it slip to Mam and Dad—then we'd be forbidden to go. Mam would probably say that it was a fool's errand. I was beginning to think that she would have been right. Making sure that the coast was clear in the landing, we shut the door and sat down on Skip's bed to plan our adventure. We checked and re-checked our flashlights and tried not to dwell on the images of dead bodies walking towards us, the Headless Horseman galloping after us with his sword, or the banshee swooping down upon us to take us off to her lair. The harder we tried not to think of things like that, the more those thoughts entered our heads and plagued us. When I get nervous I have to use the bathroom, and that night I was running downstairs to use it every five minutes, or so it seemed to me. Mam was convinced I was coming down with a stomach virus or something. First I didn't want to eat my favourite dinner, and now I was in and out of the bathroom. If only she knew!

The time had come to meet our fate. It was impossible to use the front door because we had to walk through the living room to get to it, and Mam and Dad were still up. Our only other option was to climb out Skip's bedroom window. The window swung outwards to the left, and we were able to climb onto the stone wall of Tom-Joe Queally's stables next door. He had a small yard where he kept a horse or two from time to time. We loved to feed the horse fresh grass that we pulled from our backyard. We gathered bunches of it, climbed the wall and called the horse over. The horse always seemed to enjoy the fresh grass, and Mam said that she didn't have to invest in a lawn mower because we did a good enough job ourselves keeping the grass short.

It was an easy climb onto the top of the wall, but we had to be completely quiet because the kitchen and bathroom windows were directly below us. One loud noise and someone could peek out a window and spot us escaping. That night we didn't make a sound. We jumped into Tom-Joe's yard and ran to the little door in his huge gate. After pulling the bolt back, we were able to slip out into the street. We left the door slightly ajar so as to be able to get back the way we had come, and off we walked towards the lane and the Protestant church. When we arrived at five minutes to midnight, not only were the lads there, but also it seemed like the whole town had turned out to witness the two brave adventurers embarking on a journey to certain death.

In a lonely corner of town, bordering the woods and on the bank of a small meandering river, lay the old, unused Protestant church. It was also called The Church of Ireland and was erected in 1813 in the old graveyard at the lower end of Moore Street, where the ruins of an older church, the original "church of the wood" testified that religion was nothing new to Kilrush. High, ivy-covered stone walls surrounded the church. Occasionally, goats managed to climb onto the walls and could be seen happily grazing on the sweet and succulent ivy leaves. Inside these walls, silently sleeping, were the dead founders of the town lying in a huge granite tomb with ornate roof and thick wooden doors with holes to ventilate the inside. One day I peeped through those holes and spied a dozen coffins sitting on shelves along the walls. Smaller graves of long-gone townspeople took up the remaining ground. They were old and decrepit with some dating back to the 18th Century, and many were caving in. I had enjoyed hours on different days, slowly walking around the graveyard reading the headstones and wondering what kind of life the dead people had lived. There were many infants and young children buried there, and it was with morbid curiosity that I read their names over and over again. It saddened me to think of little babies dying without having a chance to find out what living was all about. I hoped that they had been baptized before they died or else, according to the church, their souls would have gone to Limbo and they would never make it to heaven to be with Jesus. It seemed unfair to me that an innocent baby was born with original sin, and if not baptized before dying, would be banished for eternity to a scary, lonely, nowhere place called Limbo. Even at the tender age of twelve, I questioned the lack of compassion and forgiveness that would punish an innocent baby, and I secretly didn't want to believe it. *God had to be more loving, understanding and compassionate,* I thought.

    While working my way around the huge tomb in the middle of the graveyard one day, I came across a grave that had caved in. Peering into the gloom under the cracked and broken slab stone, I saw a rotted coffin and, peering straight back at me, the empty eye sockets of a skull. The fingers of a bony hand desperately reached up as if pleading for my help. There was nothing I could do. Why was the woman reaching up like that? Had she been buried alive, and in the last frantic moments before death, had she screamed in terror begging for her life? It looked that way to me, and I often prayed for her soul after that day. I wanted to believe that she was reaching for her Guardian Angel who had come to take her to heaven and she was not afraid.

The state of decay and disrepair of the graves and an active imagination on my part, made the graveyard an eerie enough place to be in the daylight and a nightmare in the dark.

Midnight came—the bewitching hour—and clouds hid the moon, casting the graveyard in deep, dark shadows. The wind blew through the trees, causing creaks and groans, which sounded to us like the voices of the dead coming back to life, and it howled and wailed like a banshee across the open expanses of the graveyard. Rain lashed against our faces as we perched on the wall, and it fell like fairy footsteps on the ivy leaves under our feet. Tombs loomed out of the shadows and, with the trick of imagination and poor lighting, appeared to be advancing towards us.

Shuddering, I whispered, "Let's stick together," before we jumped down and embarked upon one of the most terrifying experiences of my life.

Vines ran thickly along the ground to form a tangled mesh and crawled over gravestones, eating at the crumbling cement that once held the graves together. Moss and lichen clung to epitaphs and obscured the names of long forgotten souls. Weeds and briars weaved their way upward through the mesh and grew three feet tall, swaying and dipping in the wind. The only way to move was by stepping from grave to grave. As my foot touched the first slab stone, a cold shiver ran up my leg, and fingers of fear crept along my spine. It wobbled, and I screamed, leaping quickly to the next one. Vines grabbed at my ankles as if bony hands were reaching up from the graves to pull me under. On passing the tombs, I pictured open coffins on the walls and evil eyes peeping at us through the holes.

Our flashlights only illuminated what I knew was there, and I would have preferred not to be able to see at all.

"This place is really giving me the creeps," said I.

"Fuck sake, what's that?" asked Skip, as a loud screeching noise came from the trees by the main gate.

"A bloody owl I hope." And, oh, did I hope that I was right!

"Jaysus, I'm getting out of here," Skip said as he headed at full tilt back to the wall.

"Wait for me," and as I spun around to follow him, I tripped and fell on top of a grave. The flashlight went flying out of my hand and rolled along the slab stone only to disappear into the grave altogether. I was now in total darkness with just a little illumination coming from inside the grave.

The fear I felt at that moment should never be felt by anyone. In a blind panic and with a piercing scream coming from deep within me, I scrambled across the graves and clawed my way up and over the wall. A rope would have come in really handy at that point. Not even waiting to see if Skip got out okay, I ran the whole way home and straight in the front door and up to my room. Skip was a close second. Dad came up the stairs to find out what had happened, and when we told him, he burst out laughing and was chuckling to himself as he returned to the living room.

That night we heard the banshee's screech and wail. We heard the whispering of the wicked fairies in the reeds by the river and the pitter-patter of tiny feet as they ran along the wall. We saw the Headless Horseman slink into the shadows, and we held our throats. All those superstitious stories played havoc with our minds, and our hearts were frozen in fear. We realised we were not brave; we were cowards who ran from there as fast as we could never to return, even in daylight.

The crowd that had gathered to witness our demise was nowhere to be found. Apparently they feared that the banshee could fly over the wall and make off with one of them just as easily. Because of their own fears, we were held as heroes and gained a place of honour and respect among our friends, which lasted through our teenage years. Older children told younger children of our brave crossing of the graveyard at midnight, and so our reputation was handed down to the next generation of aspiring adventurers. We never did tell them the truth.

Chapter Seven
Adventures in Cow Dung

A week later, things were fairly quiet around the place. It had been pissing rain outside for days, which messed up our plans to explore. We were forced to stay inside, only venturing out to the shops or to the arcade to play pool and a few games of *Destroyer*. The arcade was nothing like the one in Ballybunnion. It was a very small sweet shop on Moore Street with a pool table in the back and a few video games. Pool cost ten pence to play, and Skip and I were fairly good and liked to compete against each other.

By mid-week I had no pocket money left and was forced to look elsewhere for something to do. So, on a rather wet and dreary Wednesday afternoon, I set off on Lightening to visit my friend Jackie Cummins, who lived in Ballynote East on a farm. Ballynote East was about two miles out the country on the way to the Kilimer car ferry.

As I set off on my bike, our dog Covey insisted on following me no matter how many times I told him to go home. He was a grand big black and brown sheepdog and had belonged to our neighbour, who used to tie him up to a pole in their backyard and leave him outside in all kinds of weather. One night during a wicked thunder and lightening storm, poor Covey could be heard howling and whimpering as he cowered next to the pole, totally tangled up on his chain. He was just a little puppy then, and Mary couldn't take hearing him cry so pitifully, so over the wall she went to rescue him. He was small enough to fit inside her jacket, and she climbed back over the wall with him tucked safely inside. The neighbours never asked for him back, so from that day on, Covey was considered Mary's dog.

When I couldn't get him to go home, I resigned myself to the fact that Covey was coming whether I liked it or not, and off I went. I had my winter anorak on and Wellington boots, which came up to just below my knees. The only part of me getting wet from the rain was my trousers, and they would dry fairly quickly by the fire in Jackie's kitchen. Her kitchen had the old fashioned fireplace that took up the entire wall. The kettle was hung over the open fire from an iron hook, and two chairs could fit inside the fireplace on either side of the fire. A huge mantle ran the length of the wall. It was just like the fireplaces you saw in the history books of old cottages in Ireland, because that is exactly what it was. Her house was very old just like mine.

I turned left at the crossroads to Ballynote East. There were a couple of farms on the right-hand side of the road before the Cummins' farm. As I cycled past one, I heard chickens clucking away in the farmyard. Covey's ears picked up, and he stopped to sniff the air and then was off over the wall chasing the chickens and scattering them in all directions. Cursing aloud, I threw my bike against the wall and vaulted over it. A white chicken was running toward a ditch in the back of the yard, flapping her wings and squawking in fear. She fell into the ditch and was sucked under the mud. All I could think of was the money I was going to have to lay out to pay for the bloody chicken if she died, so I jumped into the ditch after her. The smell of the mud was awful, and I realised that it wasn't mud at all but cow dung, and the ditch wasn't a ditch at all but a small slurry pit where cow dung is stored to be used as fertiliser for the crops.

Thankfully, the slurry pit wasn't too deep, and I only sank up to my knees. The dung, however, flowed over the top of my Wellington boots and poured inside filling them to the brim. I plunged both arms into the dung up to my armpits and frantically rummaged about trying to feel where the chicken was and all the while my long blonde hair dangled in the dung. Finding the chicken, I pulled her out and held her close to my chest, as I cleaned out her eyes and beak with one hand. She blinked at me with such a look of surprise in her eyes that on any other given day, I would have burst out laughing. At that moment, however, I was furious and made my way back to the farmhouse with Covey jumping all over me, trying to get at the chicken. Standing in the middle of his yard was the farmer with an equally surprised look on his face. He never said a word as I walked over to him with the cow dung squelching in my boots and dripping down the front of my anorak.

"Here's your fuckin' chicken," I said, as I handed her over. Grabbing Covey's collar, I dragged him out the gate and to my bike. I proceeded to break my bicycle pump across Covey's back. He was lucky the pump broke, because I was so angry I probably would have beaten him to within an inch of his life. It was a good thing we didn't make it to Jackie's house, or Covey could have killed one of her father's chickens.

I never did see Jackie that day. I got back on my bike and cycled home. Mam wouldn't let me in the front door of the house, and I had to go through Tom-Joe's yard and climb over the wall in the back to strip at the back door in the rain. Covey had to wait outside until the rain washed him off, and it served him right. No matter how hard I scrubbed myself in the bathtub, I couldn't get the smell of cow dung to leave. It was in my nostrils, under my nails, between my toes and in my hair. I soaked for what seemed like hours, until I was told to come out of the bath because someone had to use the toilet. I think I remained mad at Covey for ages after that day.

Now it isn't funny when it happens to you, but when it happens to someone else, it is another story altogether.

The following weekend, on Saturday, the sun was shining brightly and it was the perfect day to frolic in the meadow in the wood and explore, again, the ruins of what was left of the Vandeleur house. The Vandeleur Demesne, now known as the Kilrush Wood, is east of the town. The ruined Vandeleur house burned down in 1897, was demolished in 1973, and then turned into a car park and picnic area. The demesne was first planted in 1712, and John Ormsby Vandeleur built the large family home, Kilrush House, in 1808. Huge, beautiful rhododendron bushes with their large pink, purplish or white flowers, grew fifteen to twenty feet into the air, as a testament to the once splendour of the gardens surrounding the house. These very same bushes served as monkey bars, hideouts, jungle vines, and a safety net to the McCormack Gang on many an occasion.

We spent much of our time exploring the wood and knew it like the backs of our hands. One wild and crazy thing we loved to do was to climb a tall tree next to where the rhododendron bushes grew and jump from the top of the tree onto the bushes. Rhododendron is very strong and could hold our weight as we somersaulted into it. The branches were so intertwined they made a sort of net that was almost impossible to break. The first time we attempted this new and exciting pastime, Mary, Skip and I weren't so sure of the sturdiness of the bushes. We were all at the top of a forty-foot high tree, looking down and contemplating how best to test out our idea before jumping. Grace and Michael were with us, holding on for dear life to the top of the tree. (Grace was said to be the image of me with the same long blonde hair and laughing blue eyes. Michael had a head of brown curls that were the envy of every woman who paid for a perm, and blue eyes that danced with the joys of life.) They were smaller than us, so we gave poor Grace a shove, and down she went like a ton of bricks, screaming the entire time. She bounced on the top of the rhododendron but didn't go through at all. Michael was given a shove next to make double sure, and he landed the same way. There they were, rolling about on top of the bushes, laughing.

"Get out of the way," I yelled down to them. "It's our turn now."

We jumped all day, until our backsides were sore from landing on the hard branches. We showed the lads how to do it and brought our Yankee friends to the wood as soon as they arrived in town. Dennis and Kathleen Halpin lived in San Antonio, Texas, but their parents were both born and raised in Kilrush and came home every summer with their children for a couple of weeks. We brought Dennis and Kathleen everywhere with us, and they loved every minute of it. When we introduced them to somersaulting into bushes, Dennis took to it like a fish to water. He was a little daring and tried all kinds of flips and turns. One day he jumped and disappeared into the bush. I was jumping right after him and didn't stop myself in time. I came crashing through the very same hole he had made. He was hanging upside down with his ankle stuck on a branch when I landed on top of him, and we both went crashing the rest of the way down to the ground. It was utterly amazing that neither one of us was injured, except for Dennis bruising his ankle. We came crawling out of the bush laughing and giggling, much to everyone else's relief.

So it was on that Saturday afternoon in mid July when Skip and I set off for the meadow while visions of somersaults danced in our heads. Kathleen and her friend Jane McGrath came with us. We decided to take the shortcut down the lane and through Crowley's gate to approach the meadow from the other side. Skip and I whistled as we strolled behind Kathleen and Jane, enjoying the smell of the bluebells that carpeted the ground and watching the shadows dance with the sun's rays as the gentle breeze moved the treetops. What could possibly go wrong on such a perfect day?

Instead of following the little path through the trees that eventually led to the meadow in the middle of the wood, we decided to take a shortcut to the shortcut and entered the meadow by Crowley's farm. We had in fact entered Crowley's field, and the meadow was off in the distance. Not to worry, we just followed the tree line in the direction of the meadow. Over a little hill, we saw a small wooden shack with a dirt yard in front of it. Now, Skip and I were experienced explorers and this experience gave us an instinct that was wise to heed. There was something suspicious about that yard.

"I think we should go around this shack here instead of crossing the yard," warned Skip. "I don't like the looks of it."

"No way," replied Jane, somewhat annoyed that Skip should suggest the long way around.

"It looks fine to me," agreed Kathleen.

"I'm with Skip," said I.

"Suit yerselves." said Jane.

So, as Skip and I headed around the shack, Kathleen and Jane took off across the yard. All was well until they got to the middle. Suddenly cracks began to form on the top of the smooth-looking dirt, and Kathleen and Jane slowly started to sink. It was like a scene from a film where someone ventures onto an ice-covered lake only to find out that the ice is too thin, and it begins to crack. Jane looked totally panicked, and the two of them started to scream in fear and then disgust as they discovered what they were sinking into.

"Ah, shit, this is cow shit," yelled Kathleen.

"We're going to drown," screamed Jane. "Help me."

"If it gets really deep," suggested Skip, "then ye'll have to lie flat and swim to the edge like Tarzan had to do when he fell into quick sand. Cow dung is just like quick sand and will suck ye under."

"Shut up, you eejit, and help us," screamed Jane even louder.

"There's no way I'm going in there," said I.

Skip and I burst out laughing. We couldn't help it. It was such a funny sight watching Kathleen and Jane sinking into the slurry pit and seeing the looks of disgust, anger and fear on their faces. I knew bloody well how it felt and was glad beyond belief that I had heeded my instincts and taken the longer way. One day Jane had pushed Skip off a wall into a pile of nettles when he was only wearing shorts and a t-shirt, and he had gotten stung all over his arms and legs, so he had absolutely no sympathy for her and enjoyed watching her flounder about in shit.

The slurry pit was only up to above their knees, and they were able to wade to the edge and step out of it. Jane was really upset and said that her mother would kill her if she came home covered in cow dung. I suggested we go to the river where they could take their shoes and socks off and wash them in the water. They stood in the river and dunked their shoes and socks to get as much of the dung off as possible and then hung them on a barbed wire fence. Skip and I climbed some trees, looked for fish, had a scrap on the river bank, and then the four of us lay down and watched the clouds go by and waited for the socks and shoes to dry. They were still slightly damp when it was time for us to go home for our supper. We never did get to the meadow, but Skip and I agreed that it was a great day, nonetheless. I think that Jane and Kathleen would have preferred to forget it ever happened.

Family Photo, 1980

In a tree in our backyard

Outside the house

Chapter Eight
The West Clare Railway

You may talk of Columbus's sailing
Across the Atlantic sea
But he never tried to go railing
From Ennis as far as Kilkee.
You run for the train starting at eight,
You're there when the clock gives the warnin'
And there for an hour you'll wait.

From the song by Percy French, *"Are ye right there, Michael?"*

It was another gorgeous day. Puffy white clouds floated aimlessly across a corn blue sky. As we ate our breakfast in silence, the West Clare Railway beckoned us to follow the ghost tracks once again to Brew's Bridge. We knew. We had talked about it the night before and decided that it was a brilliant idea. The plans were set, the necessary supplies gathered, and we were ready for another adventure. Following the old West Clare Railway all the way to Brew's Bridge was a two-mile walk and one that we had done many times before. What we had never done before was follow the beach home. The rocky beach curved for miles around the coastline of the Shannon River: from Poulnasherry Bay, past Baurnahard Point and Skagh Point, back to Kilrush Creek. The two miles by road or ghost tracks turned into an unknown distance by beach. It was the call of the unknown that excited us, and the knowledge that a whole stretch of new territory waited to be explored.

We had coils of rope tied around our waists, penknives and flashlights dangled from our belts, pockets were stuffed with firelighters and matches to light a fire on the beach. Inside our jackets we hid sausages and bread, which we had stolen from the fridge to cook over our fire. We carried our swimsuits rolled inside our beach robes, stuffed into string bags slung over our shoulders. Brew's Bridge had the best beach around. It was rocky like Cappa, but when the tide went out a little, it was flat sand. The sand never dried, but we weren't looking for a soft spot to sunbathe on, anyway. What we *were* looking for were the oysters that buried themselves deep under the sand, leaving a telltale hole on the surface so they could breathe.

In the early 1800s the oyster beds at Poulnasherry provided industry for Kilrush, but they had been depleted from over harvesting. We ran around digging up as many oysters as we could and then counted to see who dug up the most and won. It was a fun game and, when we were done, we left the oysters in the sand to burrow their way back under to safety. Also, when the tide was out, we could walk for what seemed like miles into the water, and it wouldn't go above our knees. It was a strange feeling looking back at a distant beach surrounded by water but still not being able to swim in it. I often wondered whether I would fall into the depths if I took a few steps further, and what would be waiting for me there. That was when I would turn around and wade back to shore quickly.

I was the leader on this adventure because Mary had other things to do that day. Skip, Grace and Michael were coming with me. We walked across town to Pella Road, past the old dump, and headed to the seaweed factory at the end of Merchant's Quay. Dad had been the manager of that factory before it closed down, and we knew it like the backs of our hands. I remember visiting him at work and sitting inside his little office, spinning around and around on the swivel chair behind his desk. The office was covered in dust and smelled naturally of seaweed, which was piled in huge mounds just outside the door. The seaweed was put through a big machine that sorted out all the dirt and rocks, and then loaded onto lorries to be transported to other factories, where it would be used as an ingredient in the manufacturing of various medicines. The lorries had to be weighed on the giant weighing scale outside the town hall in the square. There were wild cats in the seaweed factory, which Dad said helped to keep the rat and mice population at a minimum. My father really loved those cats and gave them bowls of milk. He talked about them at home, had each one named, and knew their individual personalities. I don't know what happened to them after the factory closed.

Just before getting to the seaweed factory, the road to Brew's Bridge turned off to the right. It was also the road to Shanakyle Graveyard and one that was travelled upon daily during the Great Famine. Dr. Madden, historian of *The United Irishman*, in February 1851, described Shanakyle Graveyard in the following manner:

> The dead are interred every morning in a churchyard about a mile and a half from the town. The bodies are carted away without any appearance of a funeral service; no attendance of priest or parson, no pall. The coffins—if the frail boards nailed together for the remains of paupers may be so called—are made by contract, and furnished at a very low figure. The paupers' trench in a corner of the churchyard, which I visited, is a large pit, the yawning aperture about twenty feet square. The dead are deposited in layers, and over each coffin a little earth is thinly scattered, just sufficient to conceal the boards. The thickness of the covering of clay I found did not amount to two inches over the last tier of coffins deposited there.

The United Irishmen was an organization established in 1791 by elements of the Protestant and Presbyterian middle classes inspired by Wolfe Tone's claim that it would only be possible to overcome the country's problems if Catholic, Protestant and Dissenter came together, and Ireland broke the connection with England.

When Dr. Madden wrote his description of Shanaklye Graveyard, fifty people or more were dying each week. At the height of the Great Famine, the Fever Hospital in Kilrush became known as the "slaughterhouse." Famine, evictions, fever and cholera, and emigration reduced the population of southwest Clare to such an extent that it never attained its pre-famine numbers.

We chose not to take the road because behind the seaweed factory and hidden among the briars and brambles of a ditch was the beginning of the ghost tracks of the West Clare Railway. Long since dismantled but never forgotten by the older people in the town, the West Clare Railway used to transport passengers, goods, minerals, and livestock from Ennis to Miltown-Malbay. The South Clare Railway ran from Cappa Pier to Kilrush and Kilkee and was connected to the West Clare at Miltown-Malbay. The West Clare Railway was one of a network of three-foot gauge lines, which mushroomed across rural West Ireland in the wake of the 1883 Tramways Act. On May 26th 1884, an Order in Council was granted for the construction of twenty-seven miles of railway from Ennis to Miltown-Malbay. None other than Charles Stewart Parnell, Member of Parliament, cut the first sod on January 26, 1885. Mr. Parnell entered parliament in 1875 and was active in the "obstructionist" faction of the Home Rule Party. Their intention was to obstruct the day-to-day business of British parliament in order to highlight Irish issues.

Permission to build the South Clare Railway was given on August 14, 1890 and ran from Miltown-Malbay to Moyasta Cross, via Quilty, Kilmurry, Craggaknock, Doonbeg and Shragh, with branches to Kilrush and Kilkee. Both railways were commonly known as the West Clare.

Many stories were told about the West Clare. During the War of Independence, the railway employees played a prominent part in the war. They claim that they were one of the first to throw down the gauntlet to the British Army of occupation in Ireland. The locomotive crews and guards were in the front line trenches so to speak, and the stationmasters, porters, signalmen and miles men did their part when the occasion required it. Locomotive crews and guards refused to work trains when members of the Crown forces were on board. Trains were held up and raids were carried out by the IRA to examine mail, in an effort to stop information getting into the hands of the British. The railway men were the ones to give the "tip off" to the IRA when arms and other equipment were being sent to West Clare by rail

A more terrible phase in Irish history soon followed with the outbreak of Civil War, and the railway came in for more than its share of damage. A whole series of incidents occurred which often completely disrupted traffic on the system.

Of all the mishaps on the West Clare, none received as much publicity as the breakdown at Miltown-Malbay on Monday, August 10, 1896. The famed singer/song writer Percy French had a concert engagement at Kilkee that night at 8:00 p.m. and was travelling via rail from Ennis. The train was delayed for hours at Miltown-Malbay, and Mr. French was late for his concert. When he finally arrived at Kilkee, the majority of the people who had come to listen to him sing had already left and gone home. Mr. French was upset but went ahead and gave his performance for the few remaining people. He later sued the West Clare Railway for damages, stating that he did not get paid his full fee because he was late and most of the people had left. He was awarded the sum of ten pounds. Long after the other incidents on the line had been completely forgotten and the railway had passed into oblivion, the song composed by Percy French entitled *Are ye right there, Michael? Are ye right?* will remind those for generations to come that such a line as the West Clare really existed. The refrain goes as follows:

> *Are ye right there, Michael? Are ye right?*
> *Do you think that we'll be there before the night?*
> *Ye've been so long in startin'*
> *That ye couldn't say for sartin'—*
> *Still ye might now, Michael, so ye might!*

As we squeezed through the bramble bushes behind the seaweed factory and the grassy pathway where the tracks of the West Clare used to run stretched before us, those lyrics came to mind, and I began to hum the tune. As if on cue, the others joined in, and, linking arms, we marched forth singing the song at the top of our lungs. The old railway ties were long gone, but the path they took still existed, crossing farms and small country roads, and passing alongside farmhouses and the graveyard. The bridge at Brew's Bridge was no more. It used to be a railway bridge where the train crossed the road on its way to Moyasta Cross. When we got to the road, we climbed down the embankment and turned left to the beach.

The tide was way out, and many families were camped on the rocky beach while the children dug in the wet sand, splashed in the water or took turns swinging on the four swings by the edge of the car park. We were disappointed that so many people were there because it always interfered with our imaginations, where we were in the wilderness and going where no man had dared to go before. So, we decided not to stay. Virgin beach waited, and we were anxious to push on. We headed for Baurnahard Point where the beach turned sharply to the left and disappeared around a corner. As we rounded the point, Michael let out a yell of excitement and pointed to something dead that had washed up on the beach.

"What's that?" he asked me.

"It's a shark of some sort," I answered.

"What kind of a shark?" Michael persisted. "Could it be a great white shark like the one in Jaws?"

"Nah, it's way too small," said I.

"Well maybe it's just a baby one," Michael said.

"Great Whites only live in Australia," I informed him, even though I hadn't a clue myself but just wanted to sound intelligent. I was, after all, the leader and, therefore, I was supposed to know everything.

"Let's turn it over," suggested Skip.

"What if it's still alive?" said Grace, a little nervous but yet curious. Grace loved all animals and knew more about them than any of the rest of us. She spent hours pouring over the books Dad had on marine and land animals, looking at all the coloured pictures. So when Skip turned the shark over with the toe of his shoe and we got a good look at its mouth and the shape of its head, she immediately identified it as a nurse shark. She was nine years old, but we didn't even question her knowledge and accepted her identification. *She* was the expert, after all.

The baby was only about three feet long and grey in colour. Its mouth was open showing the rows of sharp teeth inside. We took turns touching its skin, which felt coarse like sandpaper. Grace wanted to bury it, but that would have taken ages and we wanted to continue down the beach and see what other interesting stuff might have washed ashore. In the end we agreed to say a prayer for its soul, and Grace kissed her fingers and gently touched the shark's head as a final goodbye. I thought she would burst into tears at any minute.

"Goodbye, lovely little shark. I'm sorry you died," she said and turned away.

An hour later we came across a big tide pool. Lying on our tummies, we looked into the water and saw crabs, sea anemones, and small fish. Skip took off his jacket and his shoes and socks, rolled up his trousers, and waded in to try and catch the fish with his hands like Tarzan could do. It was funny watching him. He stood perfectly still, bent over at the waist with his hands at the ready. When a little fish swam close, he darted his hands into the pool and brought up nothing but water over and over again.

"It looks easy on the telly, anyway," he said.

"That's because the fish are bigger," I answered him, trying to make him feel better.

"Yeah, you're right. I didn't think of that," he said. "I bet I could get one if they were bigger, too."

"I bet you could as well," I agreed.

"Watch what happens when you poke a sea anemone with a stick," said Grace. She had found a small piece of driftwood and gently poked the creature with one end.

"What are sea anemones?" asked Michael.

"Sea anemones are brightly-coloured creatures living fixed to shore rocks. They have tentacles around the mouth that are armed with stinging cells for preying on small animals," Grace recited perfectly from memory.

"Pure wah sham!" said Michael, but I could tell that he still didn't have a clue.

"Show off!" said Skip.

"They're those round jelly things with the hairy tops stuck to those rocks," I explained to Michael in simpler terms a seven-year-old could understand.

"Ah..." was all he said as he nodded his head.

When Grace poked one with a stick, it immediately pulled in its tentacles and disappeared inside itself. We had fun for a while poking them and watching them react.

The tide had turned and was on its way back in. It was also past mid-day, and we were all getting hungry and our thoughts were turning to the sausages and bread in our jackets.

"Who wants to take a swim before we eat?" I asked.

"I want to eat first and then swim," Michael answered, and Grace agreed with him.

"We can't do that," said Skip, "'cause we might get a cramp in the water. You have to wait an hour after you eat before goin' swimming."

"Skip's right," I said. "How 'bout we light the fire, then go swimming, and when we get out, the fire will be grand and hot, and we can sit around it and get dry while we cook our sausages?"

"That's a brilliant idea," said Grace, and the others agreed also.

Driftwood lay haphazardly on the beach where the river had deposited it during high tide. We gathered bundles of it and placed them in a pile inside a circle of stones. Whenever lighting fires, we took great care that the fire we lit wouldn't damage anything in nature. It wasn't much of a concern on a rocky beach, but in the Wood we had to make sure our fire was far enough away from the trees and bushes and that it was surrounded by stones so the grass wouldn't catch. We also made sure that the fire was completely out by pouring water on the embers and then covering them with sand or earth before we left it. When we had the wood piled just right around the firelighters, I struck a match, and we watched the flame catch the edge of the firelighters and spread. The driftwood was very dry and perfect food for a hungry, growing flame. In no time at all, we had a lovely fire roaring.

We quickly changed into our swimsuits, using the beach robes Mam made for us. They were light pink terry cloth with white polka dots with slits on the sides for our arms, and all six of us had one. Once changed, we carefully walked over the seaweed-covered rocks to the edge of the water. Now, I wasn't the kind of person who just jumped in. I had to test it first with my toes, then with my knees, then up to my waist, and so on until I was up to my armpits. I hated the feeling of the cold water coming over my shoulders. It made me shudder. I've been known to stay in for hours after finally getting wet, until my lips turned blue.

Skip, Grace and Michael were unable to swim, so they stayed in the shallows close to shore. I was alone in the deep water diving to the bottom, swirling around and around like a dolphin, doing somersaults and swimming like Patrick Duffy in *The Man from Atlantis*. Everything was going grand until I heard Michael and Grace talking from the shore.

"Do mother sharks stay with their babies until they're big?" asked Michael.

"No," answered Grace, "once the sacs are laid, the mother shark leaves the babies on their own."

"Do baby sharks swim along with other sharks at all then?" he further asked.

"I don't think so," said Grace. "Well, maybe if they were all feeding together."

"So, do you think that baby nurse shark we found might have been feeding with other sharks off shore from here?"

When I heard Michael ask that question I got scared and looked around me expecting to see shark fins of larger, hungry nurse sharks. A scene from the film *Jaws* popped into my head—of people's legs dangling under water and the shark coming up from the deep. I panicked and swam as fast as I could to shore and ran up the beach to the fire.

"Time to eat," I announced, so that the others would think I was just really hungry and not see that I was scared. They followed behind. We each found a skinny stick long enough to hold over the flame with a sausage at the end, and, wrapped in our robes, we sat Indian-style around the fire, slowly turning our sausages to cook them evenly. They sizzled and popped and smelled delicious. While we waited for them to cook, we nibbled on the bread or toasted a piece on another stick. Not much was said as we watched the flames dance.

While we ate our lunch, the tide came in further. It was half way up to the high tide mark, and we still had a lot of beach to follow before we were back by Kilrush Creek.

"Let's get goin' lads," I suggested. "We have a ways to go yet, and the tide is coming in quick."

Four heads ducked inside the elasticised neckline of the pink robes, and for five minutes we struggled to get dressed within the confined yet private space the robes provided. Mam called them our portable changing rooms. When done, we rolled the robes back up with the almost dry swimsuits and put them in the string bags. Skip kicked the fire over, and we piled more rocks on top of the embers and left them for the tide to extinguish.

Grace and I loved to collect lyrics to songs, and we both had a songbook the other was not allowed to see. Once I caught Grace copying the lyrics to one of my songs, and I was hopping mad and made her give me the lyrics to a song from her book that I didn't have. Every now and then, we'd tell each other how many songs we had collected. The only rule was that we had to know how to sing the song. Needless to say, we knew quite a few songs, and while we walked along the beach that day we sang. Grace would suggest a song, and then I'd suggest one, and so we continued until we couldn't think of any more. Skip and Michael joined in every now and then when they knew the words.

We were so engrossed in singing that we didn't notice we were running out of beach until we actually came to the edge of the water. I was confused and looked around us, but there was water on three sides with the tide closing in behind us. We were stranded on a little island of beach. We had reached Skagh Point whose beach stuck out into the River Shannon during low tide but disappeared at high tide. We were trapped and the only way to go was back the way we had come, before the tide came in further, and the water got too deep. After taking off our shoes and socks and rolling up our trousers, we waded through the knee-deep water, first west and then north to the shore. Poor Michael got soaked because he was so much smaller than the rest of us. Grace was a little wet, and Skip and myself were fine. It took us a half an hour to get back to where we should have been if I had paid attention. Some leader I was!

By this stage we were knackered and sat on the grassy bank of the river to catch our breath and put our shoes and socks back on. None of us wore a watch, so we hadn't a clue what time it was and didn't care much anyway. Skip was the first one to jump up and start walking around the point. The beach turned left and disappeared with Skip. A moment later we heard him yell something, and then he came running back waving his arms in the air for us to follow him, which we did.

As we turned the point, we could see a real-life shipwreck lying on its side on the beach just above high tide. My mouth fell open in amazement, and my heart began to beat faster with excitement as thoughts of pirates and treasure came to mind. We had read all the books and even seen a few films about shipwrecks and treasure, and before us now lay the opportunity of a lifetime. How many people actually got to explore a real-life shipwreck? I could tell the others were having similar thoughts as they gazed at the rotted, barnacle-encrusted hull, which leaned awkwardly to one side as if about to topple over altogether. A huge gaping hole in the hull gave evidence of the ship's demise and offered us a perfect view of the inside. The hole was big enough for me to step through if I chose to, which I did not, because the inside of the hull stunk of something rotting and was a slimy, dank, dark and creepy-looking place. Large chunks of aero board were stuffed along the inner wall of the hull and some spilled out of the hole. They were about three feet long by two feet wide by one foot thick, and Skip and I determined that they were used to help the ship float.

"Well," said Skip, "how do we go about finding the treasure?"

I knew he had been thinking along the same lines as I. *We are very much alike*, I thought, and smiled

"I'm not climbing through that smelly hole," I answered him.

"Me neither!" Skip exclaimed, with a look of disgust on his face.

"In the *Hal and Roger* books and all the other adventure books wasn't the treasure usually kept in the captain's cabin?" I asked.

"Yeah," chimed in Grace. "There might be a safe or something in there."

"How do we get all the way up there?" Michael asked, as he tilted his head back to look up at the deck high above his head.

"We'll climb up using our ropes," I answered, and I began to unravel the yards of rope I had wrapped around my waist. I knew that it would come in handy at sometime or another. A good adventurer always carried rope; it was an unwritten law and one that Sam Wise in *The Lord of The Rings* knew all about. He also knew what it was like to be caught without a rope when you needed it most. Rope, a flashlight, matches to start a fire and a penknife were the essential tools for the ardent adventurer. Skip and I had them all. We had saved our pocket money until we had enough to buy ten yards of blue nylon rope from the hardware shop on Henry Street. It was lightweight and strong and not too bulky around our waists.

Skip unravelled his rope and tied it to the end of mine to make a rope long enough to reach the railing of the deck. One rope would have done the trick, but something about tying the two ropes together made the ship appear bigger in our minds. It all added to the fantasy.

The problem now arose as to how to attach the rope to the railing so that we could pull ourselves up and over the side and onto the deck. A grappling hook would have come in real handy then, but we never thought of bringing one of those. In fact, we didn't really know what one looked like, but we did know that spies and ninjas used them to get over the high walls of fortresses.

"You're goin' to have to stand on my shoulders and see if you can tie a knot around the railing," I finally said to Skip.

As he struggled to climb onto my shoulders and I struggled to stand back up and stay steady, Michael appeared above our heads smiling in triumph.

"How the fuck did you get up there?" I asked in disbelief.

"Ah shit, stay steady Monica...fuck sake..." and down Skip fell, landing on his arse on the rocks.

We all burst out laughing, which made Skip scowl in anger, and he cursed under his breath as he got up, rubbing his arse. Michael was cracking up laughing on the deck of the ship.

"Ye'er such bloody eejits," he giggled. "I should be the leader because ye haven't a clue. Just come around to the other side and ye'll see that the deck is almost touching the ground."

Skip and I made our way around to the other side with Grace, and it was true. The ship leaned over so much that what was a high climb on one side was an easy hop-up on the other. We looked at each other sheepishly and grinned.

"Aren't we two awful gobshites, Skip?" I said, shaking my head and laughing.

The deck slanted upward at a steep angle, and we had to run up it quickly and grab onto the railing at the opposite side in order to have a look at where we had tried to climb up. On further inspection the ship became a fishing boat, and the only treasure we found were the aero boards sticking out of the hull.

"These would make great rafts," Skip said.

"Yeah, we could tie planks of wood together and then lash these underneath to help them float, and we'd have a brilliant raft altogether," I agreed.

"Let's make a raft and use it to explore the river in the woods," Grace suggested, and we all thought that would be brilliant.

"Grab as many as you can," said I. "We'll need at least six."

So, Grace and Michael carried one, and Skip and I tied two together with our ropes and dragged them behind us all the way home. It turned out that the fishing boat lay upon the beach not far from the seaweed factory and the beginning of Merchant's Quay. We carried the spoils of the day through the town and through our house and stacked them by the back door until we were ready to build our raft. That would have to wait for another day.

It was dinnertime, and we were knackered and starving. I flopped into an armchair in the living room and was beginning to take off my shoes when Grace exclaimed that she had lost her cardigan. It was a brand new one all the way from America, and Mam was mad that she had lost it so soon.

"Where did you lose it?" she asked Grace.

"I don't know," came the reply.

Dad looked at Skip and me.

"Go back and find it," was all he said.
"But it's not ours," we protested.
"Doesn't matter. Ye were in charge. Now go."
With a grumble, I retied the laces of my shoes and got up angrily from the chair and stormed out of the room slamming the door behind me. Skip was waiting outside. He was pissed as well.
"Why the fuck do we have to go all the way back?" He spat at me. "It's not our fuckin' cardigan."
"Because Grace is a fuckin' baby," I said.
We stomped off towards the seaweed factory.
"It could be anywhere," Skip said, and he was right. She could have lost her cardigan along the West Clare Railway, or at Brew's Bridge, or by the baby nurse shark, or when we looked in the tide pool, or when we went swimming, or by the fishing boat.
"We might have to walk all the way back the way we came," I said in total desperation. I was so tired and hungry and didn't want to have to repeat the whole journey again, especially now that the tide was in and it would be dark before we got back home again.
"Let's start at the seaweed factory and walk by the fishing boat and along the beach that way. She probably lost it on the beach," I said, but I really didn't have a clue where it could be.
In total silence we looked along the beach past the seaweed factory and the fishing boat, and rounded the corner by Skagh Point. The beach was gone, and the water was all the way up to the grassy edge where we had rested after doubling back when the tide cut us off, leaving us stranded on the little island of beach. There on a pile of seaweed just at the high tide mark was Grace's cardigan. We couldn't believe our luck at having found the bloody thing so fast, but we were also really angry that we had to come all the way back to find it. We spat on it, jumped on it and ground it into the smelly seaweed with the heel of our shoe, all the time screaming, cursing and yelling at it in frustration and anger. We kicked it across the beach and all the way across town to home. It didn't look new anymore.
That was the last adventure of my childhood. The following day, July 23, 1980, I became a teenager.

Chapter Nine
Deep Water

There's a place I love to go
To be free.
A wild and rocky place
By the sea.
Where the waves crash on the shore
Then recede,
Where the sun warms my face.
I pay heed
To the cry of seabirds on the
Salty wind,
To the majestic distant mountains.
I begin
To unburden all the baggage
Of the day.
I lift my soul to heaven
And I pray.

From "Deep Water"
by Monica McCormack-Sheehan

The next day I awoke early in the morning before the sun himself. I was full of excitement and anticipation for the momentous event this day would bring. You see, I was turning thirteen and entering my teenage years. These years would act as the threshold between my childhood and adulthood. They would be a time of greatest transformation for me, and I knew this and was excited. I was ready to leave my childhood behind, and I hoped that all the bad memories would remain in the past and no longer haunt me. I hoped that they would not be able to cross the threshold into my adult years.

So I decided to get up early and greet the new day and this new phase in my life at my favourite place on earth, Deep Water. Not eating any breakfast, I quietly got my bike out of the front hall and with Covey right beside me, I cycled around the Aylevaroo to Deep Water.

As I threw Lightening against the low stone wall at the top of the cliff and stepped through the gap and onto the soft heather, I looked to the East towards Money Point and could see the first light creeping over the horizon. I found my spot amongst the tall grass by the edge of the cliff, and curled up with Covey to watch the magic of a new day birthing. This was my first time, and I was awe struck at the beauty. Reds, oranges and yellows of varied hues spread throughout the clouds and set the sky ablaze pushing the blackness back for another day. The fire in the sky reflected in the serene mirror-like surface of the Shannon, dissolving the mist that lingered there, and crept towards me, lighting up the cliffs and burning into my memory. I have watched many a sunrise since then, but the thrill and excitement has never been as intense as that moment.

Once the sun burst forth from its nightly confines, it rose quickly into the sky, shining its light far into the distance so that the Slieve Mish mountains in Tralee, and Mount Brandon on the Dingle Peninsula in Kerry came into view, as did the two islands off to the west. The light that was turned on at Deep Water revealed the low cliffs covered in heather and wild flowers, the stone shed at the base of the cliffs and the cement path leading over the rocks to the water's edge. The tide was all the way in, so the river lapped against the path, and small waves crashed against the wall of the cliff. When the tide was out, you could see the steep drop at the end of the footpath and had an idea just how deep the water actually was. The river's current drifted close to shore here, and it was a dangerous place to swim especially alone. When the tide was in, the deep water off the footpath provided swimmers with a clear pool to dive into, and seaweed anchored to the rocks at the bottom floated and swayed with the current, looking somewhat like a baby kelp forest.

I uncurled myself and followed the barely visible trail through the heather to the lowest part of the cliff, where I was able to climb down the rocks to the footpath. I walked to the water's edge and then sat upon a big flat rock and gazed out over the river, listening to its quiet lapping and sucking and gurgling. My nostrils were filled with the smells of salt water, damp rocks, blooming heather and wild flowers, and a sweet breeze. I was at peace, happy and free, and eager to embrace the world and all it had to offer. I always felt this way whenever I sat upon the rocks at Deep Water, no matter what turmoil was going on in my life. It was my sanctuary, a safe haven to run to when life became difficult. I would use it often during my teenage years.

My thoughts began to drift, and I found myself thinking of *The Colleen Bawn*. Her story always made me feel so sad. She was too young to die, and she must have been so scared without her mother and father to protect her. I turned my head to the East and could make out Money Point, *Pointe an Mhonaigh*, the point of the shrubbery in Irish, where her body washed ashore. One hundred and fifty years ago, it was a busy quarry. The fine-grained rock in the quarry could be split into slabs suitable for paving, and these superior quality flagstones were sold. The folklore of the Shannon pilots tells of a ship, which left Money Point loaded with flagstones, and sank in very deep water off the point.

In June 28, 1819, a beautiful sixteen-year-old girl named Ellen Hanley disappeared from her home near Croom in County Limerick, and her body later washed ashore at Money Point on September 6, 1819. She had been murdered, and John Scanlan of Ballycahane Castle, a lieutenant in the Royal Marines and the son of one of County

Limerick's prominent families, was accused of her murder. Daniel O' Connell was his defence council, yet he was convicted and publicly executed on March 20, 1820, at Gallows Green, Singland, on the Clare side of Limerick City. Now, Daniel O'Connell was known as "The Liberator" for the role he played in the Catholic Emancipation of Ireland, and he was one of the most charismatic leaders of his generation, with a reputation that extended far beyond Ireland's shores. Still John Scanlan hung!

Ellen Hanley is remembered to this day under the name *The Colleen Bawn*, and she is buried in the O'Connell grave in Burrane graveyard. Concrete edging surrounds the grave as an attempt to stop souvenir hunters from chipping the stone. The local story is that three tombstones erected in memory of Ellen have been chipped away.

At twelve years old—well, thirteen years now—the idea of someone wanting to kill a young girl was too close to home for comfort. I could all-too-well imagine her terror when she realised there was no escape. I often prayed for her soul.

My mind drifted off to other more pleasant thoughts as I remembered the day Mary, Skip and I walked around the Alyevaroo and stopped at the top of the cliffs further down the road from Deep Water. The cliff top sloped down steeply and then either turned sharply to the left or sheerly dropped off altogether to the rocky beach twenty feet below. A thick carpet of bracken covered the top of the cliff and looked smooth, soft, and inviting. Skip jumped over the low stone wall and, sitting down on his arse, he proceeded to push himself off and slide down the bracken, turning quickly to the left before the sheer drop, using his hands to steer himself. He landed safely on some lower rocks and easily jumped down the rest of the way onto the beach.

It looked like great craic altogether, so I copied him and ended up on the beach beside him laughing.

Next was Mary's turn. She sat down, yelled, "Here I come," and pushed off. She failed to notice how we steered to the left before the drop, and so she shot straight over the edge and came sailing through the air to land on all fours on the hard rocks. A boulder lay right under her belly but her arms and legs stopped her in time before she slammed into it. Skip and I screamed, thinking she was going to be killed. Mary stood up and was pumping blood from both knees and had scratches on her hands.

"Ah, shut up, ye eejits," she yelled at us, annoyed. "Why didn't ye tell me that there was a turnoff?"

"Sure, didn't we show you how it was done?" said I, rather indignantly. "You're the eejit, not us."

"How badly are you hurt there?" asked Skip

"I've cut my knees and scraped my hands as if you're really interested," Mary responded, and she walked down to the water's edge and splashed her knees and swished her hands about in the cold water. I had an almost clean hanky in my pocket and gave it to her to wipe the blood off her knees. As soon as the blood was wiped away more blood appeared and ran down her shins.

"We'd better go home and get something for those legs," Skip said.

"Ah, it's a two and a half mile walk home and they'll be bleeding the whole bloody time. I may as well just stay here. They'll stop bleeding on their own in no time," said Mary. She ripped my hanky in two and tied it around her knees as makeshift bandages, and we continued along the beach, jumping from rock to rock, climbing the cliffs and looking in rock pools. Her knees did stop bleeding eventually, and Mam never even noticed that Mary had been injured, which was just as well because we couldn't have told her how close Mary had come to getting herself killed. Mam would have killed us herself if she found out.

My mind shifted gears once again, as I began to think about the aero board we had found by Merchant's Quay. Skip and I had drawn up plans for the raft we wanted to make and decided to begin as soon as we had gathered together the planks of wood and nails we would need. Before starting any project, not just a cycle to Ballybunnion, Dad made us present properly laid-out plans, with a list of material needed and a method for accomplishing the project. He never liked anything to be tackled half-ass. When he had any of the material we needed, he would only let us have them if he agreed the plan would work. Otherwise, he'd send us back to the drawing board.

When we presented Dad with our plans, he said that they were sound but that we'd have to find the timber because he didn't have the size we needed. He would lend us his tools as long as we put them back when we were done, and he would give us some nails. Now, all we had to do was find some old planks of timber somewhere. We thought the dump would be a good place to start looking.

I liked the dump. The old dump used to be down by Merchant's Quay at the end of Pella Road but was moved out into the country about two miles from town. When standing in the middle of the dump, piles of rubbish reached to the sky in all directions. I was surrounded by discarded treasure and never came home empty-handed. I always found what I needed no matter what that was.

When Skip and I were building a buggy to race the lads down the hill of Chapel Street with, we went to the dump to find wheels from old prams or bicycles, timber for the frame and a seat of some sort to sit on. We made the best buggy ever and won many a race the year before. The race started at the top of the hill in Chapel Drive and curved around onto Chapel Street, straight down to Moore Street. It was important to have a buggy that could turn the sharp corner at the bottom of the hill and not go out onto Moore Street and into on-coming traffic. We could only race two at a time because the footpath was only wide enough for two buggies. The winners of each heat raced each other until only one was left. Skip and I took turns driving the buggy or giving it a push off. The pusher held onto the back of the seat or the shoulders of the driver and ran as fast as possible to the top of the hill, and then let go sending the buggy flying down the hill. Great craic was had by all, and we spent hours during the summer racing until it was too dark to see. Some daring eejits even took to racing on the street itself, and many a serious accident was avoided by a last minute turn of the steering wheel by either the driver of the car or the lad on the buggy. This year, Skip crashed our buggy into Clancy's wall during the very first race and badly bent the front axle. We planned on looking for a new axle and wheels when we went to the dump to get the timber for our raft.

My stomach rumbled, reminding me that I had skipped breakfast. I said a silent goodbye to Deep Water and got on my bike to cycle the two and a half miles around the rest of the Alyevaroo past the Rock and Cappa village and home via the Fort Road. I had cycled or walked this route hundreds of times and never got tired of the beauty of the scenery. When I got home, Skip was up and, soon after eating breakfast, we headed off to the dump. Brendan O' Brien came with us and brought his baby brother's pushchair to put the timber on so we could carry it home. As we were walking down Grace Street, Brendan felt like a right eejit pushing an empty pushchair, so I got in and pretended to be a baby sucking my thumb. That just made Brendan feel even worse, and he yelled at me to get off. I took the pushchair from him and pushed it all the way to the dump. I didn't care what people might be thinking if they saw me pushing an empty pushchair. That was their business, and this was my business.

We reached the dump and set about looking for planks of timber and wheels on an axle. It made sense to split up and meet at the back of the dump. Skip took the left side, Brendan the right, and I went down the middle. There were plenty of fresh pickings that day because curbside rubbish pickup had been the day before. Piles of plastic bags with rotting food falling out lay all over the top of the mounds, and seagulls screeched in annoyance as we disturbed their afternoon snack. I kicked aside the plastic bags and rummaged through the bigger stuff underneath, looking for what we needed. All kinds of treasure showed itself to me, except wheels and timber.

When I got to the back of the dump, my arms were full of ceramic dishes and cups with only tiny chips, a stack of National Geographic magazines from a few years ago, and a perfect vase—nothing wrong with it at all. Skip and Brendan were waiting there for me, and their arms were full as well. Skip had found the wheels we needed, and Brendan had two planks of timber as well as other stuff. We filled up the pushchair and returned home. It didn't look like we'd be making a raft anytime soon and decided to just use the aero boards alone. We could put two together and lie across them and then push off and float around in the Shannon at Cappa. That's what we decided to do in the end.

In the evening after supper, we celebrated my thirteenth birthday with strawberry shortcake, which Mam made in my honour, knowing it was my favourite cake. I knew what wish to make as I closed my eyes and blew out the candles. Only time would tell if it came true or not. Lightening was my early birthday present, but Mam and Dad gave me an extra present that evening, much to my surprise. It was a lamp and a shiny new bell to put on the handlebars of my bike. I was thrilled. Skip gave me some sellotape for the office in my room (I loved pretending I worked in an office, and I collected anything that might be found in one), Mary made me a cup holder for all my biros and pencils, Kathleen knit me a beautiful scarf, and Grace and Michael combined their pocket money and bought me a bar of chocolate. It was a perfect birthday.

Chapter Ten
Relieve You

We met in the square by the town hall a few days later. It was dark out and the air was warm, as the night air in July often is. The crowd slowly gathered, as if called by the same silent piper. Skip and I arrived from Moore Street with Tara, Brendan, and Martin. Mary was already there with other lads from around the town. They leaned against the wall of the town hall or sat on the curb waiting. We stopped in front of the gathering.

"Well?" says I.

"Well," came the response from the thirty or so lads.

"Have ye picked teams yet?" enquired Skip.

"Nope," came the reply from John Foley, whose family owned a restaurant where Burton Street met the square. "We were waiting for ye."

"Grand job then. Let's get goin'," I suggested.

John and Mary were the oldest, so they were the ones to pick from the crowd of lads until two teams stood facing each other.

"Okay then, this doorway here by the men's toilets is our post," said John to his team.

"Ah, go 'way with you," said one of his lads. "The smell of piss'll make me gag."

The public toilets at the back of the Town Hall did reek of urine and something even worse. The drunks who were too legless to care or even notice the vile stench were the only ones who used them. None of John's chosen lads would hear of having their post so near the toilets.

"Alright then, how ' bout around the other side by the weighing scales?" he asked them.

"Fine with us," came their reply.

"We'll have our post by the front doors," Mary suggested to her team, and we all agreed.

Skip and I were together on the same team with Tara and Brendan and ten other lads. Poor Martin was on the other side, but he was so easy going that he just grinned at his team and pointed a finger at Skip.

"I'm goin' to catch you first," he said.

"You mean you're goin' to try," taunted Skip.

"Oh, I'll bloody well catch you alright," Martin, replied. "Just you wait!"

Mary and John flipped a ten pence coin to see whose team got to run and hide first and whose team became the hunters. The hunters' objective was to round up all the members of the opposite team and hold them at their post under heavy guard. Free members of the other team could sneak up on the post and relieve their captive teammates by placing their hands on the wall and yelling three times; "I relieve you, I relieve you, I relieve you." Then all the prisoners could run and hide again. The game sounded easy except for one thing; there was no boundary. The only place that was off limits was the wood, and the rest of the entire town was fair territory. This provided the hiding team with ample places in which to conceal themselves, and it was quite possible to stay hidden for ages if you were smart and knew the town as well as Mary, Skip and I did. The cover of darkness added to the excitement of the hunt, and oftentimes a simple game turned into a test of wits and military strategy. The hunters only became the hunted when they successfully rounded up every member of the opposite team. The game lasted for hours.

Our team won the coin toss. John picked four of his lads to guard the post. Usually the slowest or the dumbest became guards because they were hopeless at capturing the enemy. We were given to the count of twenty, and the game began. I was often amazed at how many lads got caught almost immediately. They chose stupid places to hide like the doorway of a shop or down a dead-end alley. The town was a maze of back yards, "secret" alleyways, and ruins in which to hide. As soon as the other team began to count to twenty, Skip and I took off down Henry Street with Brendan and Tara close behind.

"Where're we goin'?" asked Brendan.

"To the convent gardens," Skip answered. "We can hide in the bamboo by the main gate. No one will think of looking for us there."

"That's brilliant," Tara said.

"Let's hurry," I suggested, "before Martin sees which way we're headed. He'll know for sure where we're off to if he sees us turning down the Back Road."

"Hurry up then," Skip said.

We ran as fast as we could, keeping close to the shops and houses and staying in the shadows to avoid being seen. As we rounded the Corner House, a sweet shop on the corner of Henry Street and the Back Road, all was quiet without a person in sight. We crossed the road and ran past the girls' primary school toward the high stone walls of the convent. Huge ornate wooden gates built into a stone archway, with a stone celtic cross on top, marked the entrance to the convent's property. Smaller wooden doors, one on either side of the gate, provided access to the convent property at night when the gates were shut and locked. Cattle grating ran across the beginning of the driveway to prevent any cattle from entering the gardens beyond and destroying the lovely lawn and flowerbeds. Sr. Benedict was responsible for the beautiful landscaping. She may have been mean in the classroom, but outside she was jovial and friendly. Often, I have seen her riding her tractor mower around the vast lawns, and she always returned my wave with a smile and a wave of her hand.

The gates were locked, so we went through the smaller door on the side and found ourselves inside the convent gardens looking up the hill towards St. Mary's of the Holy Cross Convent of Mercy. It was an impressive mansion made of grey stone like the walls surrounding it. The driveway led up the small hill and curved to the right and left at the stone steps leading up to the front door. Three stories of tall, cathedral, arched windows ran the length of the mansion, indicating the numerous rooms inside. The east wing housed the convent chapel with a bell perched on the peaked roof, which was rung along with the church bells at noon and 6:00 p.m. every day to announce the Angelus.

When Colonel Vandeleur presented the Sisters of Mercy with a site to build a convent, the contract was awarded to a local builder, Mr.

Morrissey. On June 17, 1862, Bishop Flannery laid the foundation stone of the convent. Between February 1862 and April 1864, the sum of £1,858 was spent on the construction. This money had been raised through fund-raising events, while the local newspapers reported the poor living conditions and poverty of the time. *Munster News* described 1862 as an unfavourable year. There had been a bad harvest and the *News* described a harrowing picture of the awful poverty prevailing and the resulting emigration:

> That whole district of Clare down to the Land's End and far back into the country suffered .... Kilrush is the capital of the West into which labour retreats, want teeters, and feebleness crawls from many quarters as into other towns, when crops fail and the peasants' purse and donations shrivel. Through its streets every day caravans of emigrants have been passing in spring, summer, autumn and winter.

Even though the people of Kilrush suffered, still they gave of what they had to aid in the construction of the convent, and on March 30, 1864, the sisters moved in. Due to the lack of funds, only the southern section of the convent was finished, but the plans were followed and the school, chapel, and St. Timothy's Orphanage were built later on. The grounds in front of the convent were extended, and the present boundary wall was built in 1897.

It was within these walls that we sought a perfect hiding place, and we found it in the high bamboo growing to the right of the main gate. Pushing through the thick stalks of bamboo, we found a pile of grass clippings from the mower and climbed on top to sit and wait in soft comfort. We thought we had the best possible hiding place until about thirty minutes later, when we heard voices over the wall and the sound of the side door being opened.

"I bet they're in here somewhere," we heard Martin say.

"Shit, he's found us," whispered Skip.

"Stay still," I said softly. "Maybe they'll not look here."

"I would," said Skip, and he began to scoot down the grass pile and silently run alongside the wall under the bamboo.

"In here," came Martin's voice.

I took off after Skip. Brendan and Tara were not fast enough, and they made too much noise and alerted Martin and the lads with him.

"Ah, I've got ye, ye bastards!" Martin yelled.

I could hear the snapping of twigs and the rustle of leaves behind me but never looked back. I caught up with Skip at the corner of the garden. He was trying to climb the high wall. I gave him a leg up and when he reached the top of the wall, he leaned back over and gave me a hand up. Crouching as low as possible so as not to be seen, we ran along the top of the wall until we came to the end by the girls' primary school. We jumped into the bushes on the other side and took off across the playground and the front field and back onto the Back Road. Coming to the fire brigade station, we ducked behind a concrete wall to catch our breath. We could hear voices yelling on the road.

"They have to be somewhere close by," was Martin's voice.

"Where though?" asked one of the lads.

"How the fuck should I know?" Martin replied.

"Ye'll never find them," said Tara.

"Yeah, and ye'd better guard the post well, or else we'll be relieved in no time flat," said Brendan.

We now knew that Tara and Brendan had not escaped, and we would have to try to relieve them. That was a difficult thing to do. The town hall was situated in the middle of the town square and surrounded by road or car park. There was no way to sneak up on the post unnoticed unless the guards were not paying attention. We would have to come out of hiding as close to the town hall as possible, then make a mad dash towards the post, yell three times "I relieve you," while touching the wall with both hands, and then run away without getting caught. It was a daunting feat!

Our plan was simple; we would go in the opposite direction of Martin and his lads and approach the town hall from the other side of town, whence they would never expect us to come. So, we ran down the Back Road and turned left onto Tolar Street, past the church, and all the way to Frances Street. We turned left onto Frances Street and carefully made our way towards the Maid of Erin monument, where Frances Street enters the square.

Frances Street is one hundred feet wide and named after Vandeleur's wife. It was started in 1821 and finished in 1864. Vandeleur probably hoped to have it as a magnificent backdrop to the harbour when it eventually connected the lower end of the town with Merchant's Quay. It was wide enough to house a travelling carnival, and on market day, which was every Friday, vendors overflowed from the square and set up their stalls down the middle of the street. The Maid of Erin monument still stands, despite the vandalism of British soldiers during the War of Independence. The monument was built in 1903 to commemorate three young Fenian men—Allen, Larkin and O'Brien—who were executed for their attempted rescue of two Fenian leaders, during which a policeman was accidentally killed.

We made our way to the iron railing around the monument and ducked down to stay out of sight. We slowly raised our heads to peer over the railing by the corner of the monument and could clearly see the town hall. The enemy's post was on the opposite side of the town hall and out of sight. No guard was posted at the corner of the building to watch for a sudden surprise "relieve you" attempt from behind. We scanned the square and branching streets for signs of any of the lads from the other team, but all we saw were a few people coming out of Coffey's Fish and Chip shop, and some teenagers hanging around Burke's shop on the north corner of Frances Street and the square.

"Let's go," said Skip.

We made a mad dash across the square and flattened ourselves against the south side of the town hall by the men's toilets. They stunk! We inched our way along the wall, and Skip took a quick peek around the corner to assess the situation.

"They've captured most of the lads except for Mary, and Katie O' Leary," Skip whispered, "and Martin is standing guard with about six other lads."

"Okay then, let's do it this way; you go around first and relieve the lads, and while Martin is busy trying to catch you, I'll come behind and finish the job," was my suggestion.

"Sounds like a plan," Skip agreed, and away he went.

I heard the uproar as Skip ran to the post and yelled "I relieve you," but he only got to say it twice and was off running with Martin and all six of the lads hot on his heels. I crept around the corner to finish the job, and the lads on my team scattered to the four winds hooting and hollering in glee. Skip and I had agreed to meet up again in Chapel Drive, and when I arrived, there he was sitting on Shannon's wall, laughing and out of breath. He had led Martin and the lads on a merry chase. We walked down the lane behind Clancy's house and found a great hiding place under the ivy on the ledge of a ruined house behind O'Donnell's. We lay there in silence for a long time and almost fell asleep.

"This is boring," Skip said. "Let's go and see what's going on."

When we walked back up to the square, there was no one around. All the lads had gone home to bed, and the game was over.

"We must have won," said I.

"Wonder if they ever caught Mary?" Skip answered.

"Let's go home and find out," was my reply.

So, off home we went. Coming through the doors into the living room, we spied Mary sitting on the couch by the storage heater, drinking a hot cup of tea and eating Jaffa cakes.

"Where did ye disappear to?" she asked us. "The game's been over for ages."

"Did they catch you?" we asked.

"Nope," came Mary's proud reply, "Katie and I hid in the sheds behind her backyard and had a grand time chatting and eating Taytos."

"Martin almost caught us in the bamboo in the convent garden, but we escaped and relieved everyone. Then we hid in the lane behind Clancy's," I informed her.

"Well, then we won," Mary, announced.

Oftentimes, the game ended without any clear victory and with each side remembering the outcome in their favour. It really didn't matter who won because the fun was in the playing of the game and not in its outcome. The craic was mighty and that's all that mattered.

Chapter Eleven
Cappa

One mile from Kilrush and on the banks of the River Shannon was the little village of Cappa, where we went to swim and dive off the pier. There are two roads leading to the village: the main Cappa Road and the old Fort Road. The Fort Road was the original road to Cappa, and the ruined fort on Cappa Hill stood as a silent reminder of the colonial past when the British military used the fort as their barracks. We mostly took the Fort Road because it was quicker for us, and it was a quieter, more peaceful way, passing farms and country homes.

Cappa Pier was the most important factor in the development of Kilrush. It has changed little since it was first constructed in 1764. Samuel Lewis, in his book *A Topographical Dictionary of Ireland*, 1837, described the pier to be of very solid construction protected by a sea wall of great strength and with water deep enough to admit large ships.

The village itself was a tiny T-shape of houses, Pine's shop, the Galley Inn, and the Pilot House. On the top of Cappa Hill, before the entrance to the village, was the ceramic factory, which made beautiful crockery. Behind this factory was a massive pile of broken or otherwise imperfect dishes, cups, saucers, plates, vases, and so on. It was every child's dream. Skip and I, on many an occasion, went there to break at random as many cups and plates as we could. We tried to find the more perfect ones and piled them at our side. Then choosing a target, we took aim and let them fly, enjoying the sound as each piece of crockery exploded upon impact with the target or the ground. There is a certain sweet music in the sound of breaking dishes that is lost when the dish is broken by accident, and it just happens to be your mother's best dish. So, here on the pile of discarded and unwanted dishes we could listen to the symphony they created as we afforded them a befitting end to their brief existence. Sometimes, we found an accidental throwaway, and this we proudly brought home to our mother as an offering to replace something of hers we had broken in the past or were sure to break in the future.

One day, Michael came across a beautiful serving dish with a lid that looked like a hen sitting on her nest. For some reason it had been discarded, although we couldn't find any fault with it except that it had never been painted or fired in the kiln to give it that lovely shiny look. Michael was an artist and he saw the possibilities of what this serving dish could look like when he painted it. So, he took it home and after some time presented Mam with a gorgeous brown hen sitting on a nest of pale yellow straw with two yellow chicks tucked under each wing. He had glazed it to make it shine. Although Mam could not put food in it because it wasn't finished inside the proper way, she put it over the range in the kitchen for everyone to admire, and there the hen still sits. I was very impressed with Michael's talent, and he only seven years old. He went on to become a phenomenal artist in his own right.

Ships passed up and down the Shannon River on a regular basis, bringing cargo up to Foynes and Limerick, or carrying it back down to the Atlantic and out to the rest of the world. As with in any river, it is vital to have knowledge of rocks, sand bars, or other obstacles in the Shannon that might endanger the ship. The Shannon River was not without its dangers. Only a few highly skilled local boatmen knew how to navigate the Shannon Roads, a name given to the deep and safe channels of the river. These were the Shannon Pilots, and they operated out of the Pilot House directly across from the pier. The pilot boat was docked at the pier when not in use. It was a small black boat with a white wheelhouse. Michael Scanlon was the senior pilot. His family was one of the last to leave Scattery Island where Michael grew up, and he now lived in a row of small houses along Merchant's Quay. He was a lovely man and my good friend, and I loved listening to his stories in front of the fire in the pilothouse, sipping a cup of tea he made for me, and nibbling on a chocolate Gold Grain biscuit. The pilots on duty waited in the pilothouse for a call from a ship entering the estuary and needing a skilled navigator to bring the ship safely up the Shannon Roads. I often sat with them as they waited, hoping to be invited along for the ride when the call came through, and while we waited, Michael told his stories. He was very old with sparse grey hair, a round weather-beaten face, and gnarled hands. Despite his age, he was immensely strong with a keen eye for the river and an innate knowledge of the weather. The younger pilots listened and learned from him. He talked about his life on Scattery Island, accidents on the river, people drowning, storms, and always about his wife Alice, whom he loved so much.

In early August, I was visiting Linda McFadden who lived in Cappa. She was related to Michael Scanlon, as most of the people from Scattery Island and Cappa were related. We just happened to be in the pilothouse when a call came in from a Greek ship requesting a pilot to bring her up the Roads. The McFadden family were intimately involved in river life, and Linda had been on the pilot boat many times. When she asked Michael if I could come along, he looked me intently in the eyes as if sizing up my character. I was an outsider, a Townie, and I suppose he was trying to determine if I had sea legs or if I'd be likely to get motion sickness and be a nuisance. I was determined not to be and tried to convey that thought to Michael through my eyes. He understood. Winking at me, he gave the okay, and I jumped up and down in glee.

"Are ya sure you're mother won't mind ya comin'?" He asked.

"Oh no," I lied straight-faced. *She'd only bloody well kill me flat out if she knew*, I thought.

"Well then, lend a hand here, and we'll be off."

I helped him carry some stuff down the stairs and over to where the pilot boat was tied up by the pier. As we walked, Michael told me the rules of his boat.

"You're not to touch anything," he warned. "Stay out of our way, and listen to what you're told. If you give me any trouble, I'll lock you in the hold 'til we get back."

"I'll stay clear of you then," said I, and I meant every word of it.

I didn't want to spend this whole adventure stuck below deck, just for the thrill of touching a button or pulling a lever out of curiosity.

"They'll be no going to the loo and nothing to eat either, and we'll be gone for a while," he warned.

"That's all right. I'm not hungry and I can hold it in if I have to go," I replied, determined not to let anything stop me from going. "How long will we be out?"

"A few hours at the most, I'll wager." came his answer as he quickly backed down the iron ladder to the boat that bobbed in the low tide and banged against the side of the granite pier wall. Tires dangled from the side of the boat at intervals and acted as a buffer between the pier and the black hull. I glanced over the edge of the pier at the twenty-foot drop to the deck below, and I have to admit I was scared. I had never done this before but didn't want to let on. Linda was next and climbed down the ladder with great ease, followed by her older sister Noreen, who decided to come along as well. It was now my turn, and all eyes were upon me as I threw one leg over the edge and found the first rung of the ladder. I closed my eyes, took a deep breath, and trusted in God for my safe landing, which He granted. Another pilot was already on board, had the engines turning over, and was on the ship-to-shore radio with the captain of the Greek ship. Linda and Noreen's younger brother Christy cast off, and the boat slowly chugged away from the pier and headed out to the open river.

I looked out the window of the wheelhouse as the pier was left behind and we got closer and closer to Scattery Island. I had never been on the Island or even close to it but only knew it from the shore. The round tower, abandoned village, ruined churches, and the school house were clearly visible, and I thought I would give anything to be able to explore that island with Skip. We would be in our glory!

As the pilot boat entered the open water of the Shannon Estuary, the wind picked up and choppy water turned into ten-foot swells. We climbed the crest of the waves and plunged into the troughs. Linda, Noreen and I were sitting on top of the cabin, holding onto the metal railing and laughing in pure delight as the wind whipped our hair and spray drenched our faces. We plunged once again into a trough, and

the boat rocked to one side, sending Linda over the edge. She was almost swept overboard completely but held onto the railing with one hand. Noreen and I grabbed her jacket and pulled her in. The wheelhouse door slid open, and Michael poked his head out.
"Get down below," he yelled into the howling wind.
"Awww," the three of us complained, but we did as we were told. The cabin below deck smelled of diesel and was used for storage of rope, life vests, tools, oil and gasoline, lamps, and extra tires. As the boat pitched, we tried to stand in the middle of the floor with our legs spread apart to hold our balance. It was difficult to do, and often we were sent sprawling across the cabin. The pitching and rocking and smell of diesel began to affect my stomach, and I had to sit down. I struggled to keep my breakfast inside. Michael's voice could be heard talking on the radio to the waiting ship. The next minute, he yelled down the hatch that we were putting to shore until the rough sea subsided.

We put in at Carrigaholt, which is a fishing village facing east into Carrigaholt Bay. There are a couple of stories as to how it got its name. The first, *Carraig an Chabhaltaigh*, rock of the fleet, may refer to the small fleet of seven Armada ships that found shelter in the Mouth of the Shannon in 1588. The second, *Carrick-an-oultage*, or the Ulsterman's Rock, after a native of County Down who supposedly built the castle there on a low rocky headland overlooking a fairly modern pier. Several fishing boats operate from the pier, and during the summer months it is a popular port of call with boatmen. Its position on the West Clare peninsula makes it a great place for tourists who love the Rent-an-Irish Cottage holiday opportunity. There is a grand sandy beach east of the village, and O'Curry College of Irish is nearby, which enabled Carrigaholt to keep its reputation as a mini-*gaeltacht*, although it hasn't been recognised as an all-Irish speaking part of the country since 1891.

The Irish language, of which Scottish Gaelic and Manx are dialects, is of Celtic and ultimately Indo-European origin, and had been spoken in Ireland for 2,500 years. It only underwent serious challenge with the introduction of substantial communities of English speakers, after the English invasion in the late 12th century. By the early 17th century, the native aristocracy—the principal patrons of Gaelic culture—had been overthrown, and the language lost its ascendancy. The early 19th Century saw more Irish speaking people in Ireland than ever before, but they were the poorest sections of society, and Irish was being abandoned at an accelerated rate long before the Great Famine, as the underclass sought to gain social and economic advancement. The *Gaeltacht* is now the only remaining Irish-speaking area in Ireland. Compulsory instruction of Irish in schools has attained only limited success. O'Curry College of Irish in Carrigaholt played an important role in keeping the Irish language alive in Ireland.

The strong wind dropped to a stiff breeze on land, and the sun was warm. Michael told us to go on off to the village down the road a bit to find a toilet and something to eat. I had no money, so he gave me the few coins in his pocket. I kissed him on the cheek, which seemed to embarrass him, and off I went. There was nothing going on in the village, and not a soul could be seen. We found a tiny shop, which sold just about everything you could possibly need or want, and bought ourselves some bags of Taytos and cans of Fanta. We sat on a bench overlooking Carrigaholt Bay and ate in silence, enjoying the view. One little pub was open and even had a few customers, and the bartender let us use the loo in the back. Our business done, we set off to explore the castle ruins and play along the rocky beach by the pier, staying close enough to be able to hear Michael's call to come back on board. It was a few hours before we heard him yelling our names.

Michael certainly knew his weather; the wind had died down completely, and the river was calm once again. We quickly made it to the Greek ship that waited just a few miles further down the river not far from Loop Head. It was the biggest ship I had ever seen and dwarfed the pilot boat as we pulled alongside her. A rope ladder was dropped over the side, and the younger pilot climbed up it like a monkey and disappeared over the rail of the ship, high above our heads. A few sailors waved down to us, and we returned the wave. The pilot took over the helm and steered the ship safely up the river past Money Point. We were waiting for him there in the pilot boat to take him back to Cappa, and the ship continued on in safety to its destination. A few hours had turned into the whole day, and I couldn't wait to get home and tell Skip where I had been. When I did, he was hopping mad that he missed such a fabulous adventure.

The two of us went back to Cappa the next day with our aero boards to test our theory of using them as a raft, lying across two of them and then floating around in the river.

Behind the sea wall is a rocky beach for bathers. It has a men and women's changing room, which never seemed to smell that good, and a concrete footpath leading down the beach to the water's edge. Whenever the weather was dry, the beach was crowded mostly with young children and their parents. The older children and teenagers preferred to dive off the pier or swim from the pier across to the boat slip about one hundred feet away. We held diving competitions and relay races and took running jumps off the pier to see who could produce the biggest splash, yelling, "Yipee, Yapee, Yahooee."

We decided to launch the aero boards from the beach where it was shallow, in case we were unable to stay on top of them and fell into the river. It wouldn't have mattered much with me, but Skip couldn't swim yet. It proved difficult to keep two aero boards together while climbing on to them, and we fell off constantly until we got the hang of it. Once safely on top, we used our hands as mini paddles and moved along the shoreline looking over the edge of the front aero board and into the river. We saw fish swim by, crabs run along the bottom, and we watched the seaweed sway with the current. Using our hands, we propelled ourselves forward and around and around as fast as possible. So engrossed were we that we failed to notice how far out into the river we were drifting, until Skip fell off trying to reposition himself on one of the boards. He went straight under. We were close to the end of the pier, and the water was very deep. He came back up sputtering and thrashing his arms about. I was a very weak swimmer and knew that I wouldn't be able to save him.

"Grab onto one of the aero boards," I yelled in panic.

"I can't reach 'em," he answered, and I noticed that the boards were beginning to float away. I propelled myself over to the closest one and pushed it towards Skip who was coming back up for the second time. He was able to grab onto it with one hand and tried to swim with the other hand, but the board was too thick and he lost his hold and slipped under again. When he came back up, he grabbed on with both hands and let his body float under the aero board, so that he was on his back looking up at the sky. Kicking his legs, he slowly made his way back to shore, much to his own relief and mine. It was a close call. You'd think it would have scared him away from using the aero boards again, but not Skip.

For the rest of the summer, we floated on those aero boards every chance we got. We brought snorkels with us, so we could get a really good view of the bottom. We didn't stay in shallow water either. The fact that Skip figured out how to hold on to the aero board and float back to shore only gave him more confidence, and so we floated off the pier and over by the Rock. The only place we didn't dare go was to Deep Water because of the strong current close to shore there. The wrecked fishing boat by the seaweed factory did have treasure in it after all, and it only took our imaginations to see that the aero boards gifted us with the precious treasure of happy memories.

Chapter Twelve
The Fields

Dusk is the mystical veil between our world and the fairies'. The setting sun gives the warning that soon all will change in the fields, and so beware. We looked for the signs and when they appeared in the sky we knew it was time to return home. In the second field behind Chapel Drive, on top a small round hill, was a perfect circle of gorse bushes. It was here that the fairies were said to dance under the moonlight before setting off to play their mischief on unsuspecting humans. It was here also that we played numerous games of hide and seek, always careful to leave before the fairies awoke.

Safe passage was not guaranteed in daylight, however, for the fields were home to bloodthirsty greyhounds that were said to have ripped a dog apart. When the sound of their baying came on the wind, it was time to run for our lives. It was said that fresh meat was all they would eat, and children were easy prey.

One afternoon in mid-August, Skip, Grace, Michael, and I set off to play in the fields. It had been raining for days—this was the first day of sunshine in a week—so we wanted to make the most of it. Much of the fields were soggy mud or large ponds of water from flooding. Skip had told his friend Liam Sullivan that mackerel could be caught in these ponds after very heavy rain because they were really deep then. Liam was gullible, and Skip swore that he believed him.

When we got to the gorse patch, the game began. We played on our hands and knees and chased each other in and around the bushes. It was Skip's turn to find us and he cheated by standing up in the middle of the circle to get a better view of the surrounds. Something caught his eye as he glanced to the north, and he stopped playing.

"Mon, what's that over there on that hill?" he asked me.

I stood up then to see what he was looking at.

"I don't see anything," I answered him.

"Over there next to that tall oak tree right in the middle of the hill," he insisted.

I looked again and could make out what appeared to be a small rock.

"Looks like a small rock to me," I offered.

"Not that small 'cause it's far away," he said.

"Well I don't know what it is. Now, are you playing or not?"

"I want to go see it," he answered and began walking in that direction.

"Wait Skip," I said. "What about the greyhounds?"

"I don't hear their baying, and anyway, I don't think that story is true at all."

"What if it is, and we get caught?"

"Then we'll have to stay absolutely still, because greyhounds like to chase their prey like they do in the greyhound races."

"That's just a mechanical rabbit on a track."

"Yeah, but they don't know that."

"True enough."

"Are you comin' then?"

"Alright. Grace and Michael, game's over. Let's go."

Grace and Michael jumped up from where they were hiding and came running after us. When we told them where we were going, they got scared.

"But the greyhounds will tear us apart if they catch us," protested Michael, and Skip told them about staying still and not running away.

"What if it doesn't work?" Grace asked, with uncertainty in her voice.

"Then ye can hide behind me and I'll protect ye," I said.

"How're you goin' to do that?" It was Michael's question, and he wasn't convinced that I would be much protection against a pack of man-eating hounds.

"While they're ripping her apart, we'll make a run for it," was Skip's suggestion, and he gave me a wink. Didn't the other two go along with it! They were bloody well ready to sacrifice me to save themselves. I wasn't too sure what to make of it, but at least they had stopped asking questions and were following along, so I kept my mouth shut.

We jumped over the stile between each field until we got to the one with the high hill and the mysterious rock on top. Stiles are an arrangement of steps made out of wood or piles of rocks for people to climb through a gap in the bushes that mark the boundary of each field. They eliminate the need for people to open a gate and so reduce the risk of cattle escaping. The south boundary of the field we wanted consisted of a high ditch with thick brambles and intertwining tree branches acting as a further barrier. The ground was wet and muddy from the previous few days' rain, and it was a tough climb to the top. We used the tree branches as ropes and cut at the bramble thorns with sticks. Despite the difficult climb, we all made it to the top with no assistance from each other. Sticking out of the ground a few meters from us was a chimney. It was rectangular in shape and made from grey stone. We couldn't believe it and ran up for a closer inspection.

"It's a bloody chimney!" Skip said in disbelief.

"What's it doing in the middle of a field?" I asked.

"Let's throw something in and see how far down it goes," said Grace.

So Grace and Michael looked around for stones to drop down the chimney. Skip took his flashlight from the hook on his belt and shone it down the shaft, but it wasn't powerful enough to illuminate inside. I added the light from my flashlight to see if it made a difference, but it didn't. Michael came back with two stones and threw them down the chimney, and we heard a sharp sound as they hit rock far below.

"This chimney goes down deep," Skip said.

"I wonder what's down there," I added.

"Could it be an underground house?" asked Grace.

"Yeah right!" Skip and I said together.

"Well it could be," she insisted.

"Then where's the front door, or a way in?" Skip asked her.

"Maybe at the bottom of that ditch we just climbed up," and after she said it, Skip and I looked at each other and took off towards the ditch. We slid down the mud embankment, paying no attention to the prickly thorns that tore at our clothes. When the other two caught up, we were standing in front of the ditch trying to figure out where the door might be. It was well hidden behind trees and bushes, and it took us a good half hour to find it, but find it we did. There built into the face of the ditch was a stone wall with a small square entryway and a little window to one side. There were no windowpanes or wooden door. I took out my flashlight again and, leading the way, stepped through the entrance and into a dark and damp room. On the far wall was a fireplace with the two stones Michael had thrown down in the hearth. Narrow stone steps led up and around the fireplace but, upon further inspection, we found the stair didn't go anywhere. It just ended at the top step and no matter how hard we looked, we couldn't find a secret handle or any other way to open the rock wall. We determined that it must have been an escape hatch. Some debris and animal droppings were on the flagstone floor, but otherwise the house was in excellent shape for its age, and it had to be very old indeed because no one had ever mentioned it before. In a small town like Kilrush, stories about an underground house would have been circulated, unless the people who knew of its existence were long dead. We came up with theories of our own as to why it was built, and the role it played in the history of the area. One theory was that it was a bomb shelter, and another one was that it was used by the IRA as a hideout during the War of Independence and then again during the Civil War. Whatever its purpose had been, no one had set foot inside for a very long time. The entanglement of bushes and trees had not been disturbed and had completely obscured the doorway.

At last, a real hideout! We could light a fire and not have to worry about anything catching fire around it. We could come here on rainy days, cook sausages, play games, tell ghost stories, or do whatever we wanted to do. It would be our home away from home, and we decided to come back the very next day with supplies to leave there. Back outside, we started to walk towards home to tell Mary about our find. Suddenly, faint in the distance, could be heard the distinct sound of hounds baying. A look of complete panic flashed in Michael and Grace's eyes, and they clung to me.

"Let go of me, ye eejits," I yelled, as I pried their fingers from my sleeves and yanked my jacket free. I wasn't about to be the scapegoat on this adventure because that meant a certain, very painful death. I did, however, grab Grace and Michael's hands, and we ran as fast as we could across the sodden slippery fields. The baying got louder and louder and looking back, I saw the pack of hounds leap down the high ditch in two bounds and close on us.

"Stop running," I screamed. "They're gaining on us."

Everyone stopped and turned to face their end. Bravery and responsibility urged me to shove Skip, Grace, and Michael behind me, and I put my arms out and started yelling at the dogs in anger. The other three clung to me sobbing in fear. I wanted to cry myself, but I was too stubborn to go down without a fight. We were quickly surrounded. I karate kicked at the hounds, waving my arms in wild gestures over my head, and all the while I cursed and screamed at them in a rage. The hounds looked confused and stopped their loud din, and they looked on at the crazy young girl who had obviously lost her mind.

"Don't be afraid, they won't hurt you at all," came a deep voice from behind me.

"Then call them off," I angrily demanded, as I turned to see a middle-aged man dressed in a dark brown tweed jacket, brown trousers tucked into black Wellington boots, and a tweed cap on his head. In his hand was a walking staff of polished Blackthorn. He gave a barely audible whistle, and the greyhounds left us and obediently surrounded him with tails wagging, tongues hanging out, and big grins on their faces. They were enjoying themselves.

"I'm sorry ye were frightened by my dogs, but they wouldn't hurt a fly," the man gently said.

"You mean, they're not goin' to rip us apart?" Michael asked, still hiding behind my back and clinging to my jacket.

"Now why would they want to do that for?" he asked us.

"Well, don't they only eat fresh meat and hunt their prey?" Skip asked back.

"Not bloody likely," the man answered, chuckling in mirth at the idea of his hounds hunting for food. "They're racing hounds, and I feed them special dry food at home. They don't eat any meat at all."

"I told you the rumour was just another bloody lie," said Skip.

"Well, you believed it too," I insisted.

Just then, Grace slipped out from behind my back.

"Then they're just nice dogs having some fun." she said.

"They're out for a bit of exercise," the man agreed. "I let them run in the fields. It's great practise for them."

"Have they ever won a race?" Grace asked, interested.

"Yes, this one here has won two races in Limerick, and this girl won a race last month in Galway. They are the parents of these five puppies who are not old enough to race yet."

"How old are the puppies?" I asked, because none of the dogs looked like puppies to me.

"They're only eight months old and love to run about and play." was his reply.

"So, they only wanted to play with us then and not eat us." Grace stated.

We looked on the greyhounds differently then; all of our fear evaporated, and we began to pet the puppies as they jumped all over us. The rumour had been false, and we had run in fear for no other reason than that we believed what we heard without seeking the truth for ourselves. A true adventurer finds his own path through life and forms his own opinions from experience, not from what other people say. This knowledge in action becomes wisdom in time. We had let fear cloud our intuition and had not acted wisely at all. That was the last time I ever believed a rumour.

We saw the signs in the sky that night was approaching and were tempted to stay in the fields to see if the stories about the fairies were true. Those stories weren't just rumours, however, but myths and legends going back hundreds of years, and we were inclined to believe that maybe there was some truth in them. But we had had enough adventures for one day so headed home instead.

As we walked through the last field before Chapel Drive, there was Liam Sullivan standing at the edge of the flooded field casting his fishing line into the deep pond created by the floodwater.

"What are you doing?" I asked, puzzled.

"Catching some mackerel," came his answer. He believed Skip's rumour, and Skip decided to set Liam straight before he made an eejit of himself in front of the other lads.

"I was only messing with you when I said mackerel were in these ponds. Sure, mackerel only live in salt water. There's no fish in there at all."

"You fucker," Liam yelled at him, and he gathered up his pole and line and took off in anger.

We burst out laughing. Whoever started the rumour about the greyhounds would probably laugh at us as well. So it was decided that it just wasn't a good idea to believe in rumours or to start any ourselves.

Chapter Thirteen
Rawkin' Apples

It was the last Friday in August, and the day dawned grey and cold and wet. I missed the dawn and slept straight through to noon, only opening my eyes once to glimpse the colour of the sky out my bedroom window around nine o'clock. It occurred to me that this was the last chance I had to sleep late on a weekday for a long time, so I had better stay in bed and enjoy it while it lasted. So I did just that. When I finally staggered down the stairs and into the kitchen at twelve o'clock, I had a pounding headache from too much sleep. Skip and Mary were sitting at the kitchen table eating their breakfast and drinking cups of hot tea, and I joined them. School was starting on Monday. For Skip and Mary it wasn't an exciting prospect because they were going to the same school again, but I was starting secondary school, and I couldn't wait. We talked about all the fun we had had that summer and decided to go out with a bang. What could we do for the grand finale? There was only one thing that we hadn't done yet, and that was rawkin' apples from Bonnie Dune's orchard.

"That's a brilliant idea," Mary said, after hearing my suggestion.

"Yeah, we can bring plastic bags with us and fill them up, and maybe Mam will make some apple tarts," Skip added.

"Let's go and ask all the lads if they want to come with us," I further suggested, "and then we'll have brilliant craic altogether."

"Grace and Michael will come for definite, and we can all meet on the wall across the street at two o'clock," Mary said, and off we went to our respective friends to see who wanted to come rawkin' with us. No one wanted to come, however, so it was the McCormack gang who set off that day on the final adventure of the summer.

Bonnie Dune's house was on Frances Street, and her backyard stretched all the way back to the little river that meandered past the Protestant Church, under the bridge on Stewart Street, behind all the back yards of Moore Street and Frances Street, and eventually made its way to the Shannon River and out into the Atlantic Ocean.

We knew how to get into her backyard from the river, and we also knew that she had the best apple trees in town. On the opposite bank of the river behind Frances Street, there was a small wood that we called the Secret Wood where the sewage treatment plant was located. We could get to the Secret Wood by cutting through fields from either Stewart Street or Cappa Road at the end of Frances Street. I wanted to take the Cappa Road way and strongly urged everyone to follow me. As we walked around the corner from our house, Mary argued that Stewart Street was the faster way to go, and that it made no sense to her to go all the way down Frances Street when Stewart Street was closer.

It made perfect sense to me. I didn't want to go anywhere near the part of the wood that housed the sewage treatment plant. It was a bad place and bad things happened there. You had to run as fast as you could to escape, and then you couldn't find the way out and had to climb over a really high red iron gate with sharp spikes on the top. First you had to throw your dog over the gate because you could hear him yelling that he would kill the dog if you didn't stop. What if he meant to kill you? When you climbed the gate and jumped down the other side, you could hear the gate rattle as he climbed after you, and then you panicked and had to run even faster across the field. The easy way out of the field was too far to the right, and he could cut you off as you came back left to Stewart Street, so you ran straight to the bridge on Stewart Street. After climbing on to the top of a fence by the river, you had to stand on tip toes to reach the top of the bridge wall, all the while hearing him calling to you to stop, and threatening your dog as he got closer and closer. Leaving the dog to take care of herself, you managed to scramble over the top of the bridge and onto Stewart Street sobbing in fear. Looking back, you saw him turn down the small lane by the Slaughterhouse, and you didn't stop running until you came crashing through the door of the living room to safety. That's what happened when you went into the wood from Stewart Street, and I did not want to go through that again.

My private turmoil of remembering went unnoticed by everyone else, and while I was once again frantically escaping in my mind, the decision had been made to take the shorter way through hell. I never talked about what had happened to me, and if I changed my mind and backed out now they would want to know why. So with dread in my heart, I reluctantly agreed to follow along.

As we turned the corner and crossed Moore Street heading towards Stewart Street, we met Tommy McGuire who was riding his small blue bike. Tommy looked bored and asked us where we were going. Before Mary, Skip or I could tell him "nowhere," Grace and Michael spilled the beans and told him we were going rawkin' apples. He begged to come along too, and even though we told him to buzz off, he followed behind us on his bike and wouldn't leave us alone. Tommy wasn't one of the lads, and we had no idea if he would be able to keep up with us, or if he had the guts to cross the river and rawk apples. We didn't want anything ruining our last great adventure of the summer.

He was persistent though, and we had to lift his bike over the low part of the wall and hide it in a bush in the field. The whole way across the field he annoyed us with questions.

"How do we get across the river?" was one.

"There's a kind of wall that goes from one side to the other and it's pointy on top so you have to be careful and not fall off into the river or else you'll drown," Mary exaggerated.

The wall was about three feet wide at its base and tapered at the top to about three inches in width. The brave ones who weren't afraid of falling into the river were able to tightrope walk across the wall to the other side, but most of us were afraid to do that, so we straddled the wall and using our hands as leverage, were able to slide our arses across the wall to the other side.

One time, a year ago, we were playing Tarzan by Monkey's Island, which was in the middle of the river closer to Stewart Street. We tied a rope to a tree limb overhanging the river, and the plan was to swing from the rope across the river and land on Monkey's Island. Mary and I weren't sure if the rope was tied properly, so we elected Michael to be the guinea pig and test it for us. Being the youngest of the McCormack gang, he was made to carry all our stuff, and test what we were unsure of. We liked to think of it as a form of initiation, but it was really because we were mad at Mam for making us drag him along with us all the time.

In our imagination that day, the river was a raging torrent swiftly sweeping everything in its path to the brink of a waterfall before plunging into oblivion, and Monkey's Island was the home to man-eating apes lurking in the bushes, waiting for their unsuspecting lunch to come swinging through the air and land in their lair. Michael, only six at the time, truly believed in our game, and when we made him be the first to swing across the raging torrent and land among the killer apes, he was petrified. Desperate to be accepted into the most elite gang of all, the McCormack gang, he slowly grabbed the rope and held on for dear life, as Mary pulled him backwards and upwards and let him go with a shove. He went sailing through the air screaming, but the scream was short-lived as the rope came undone and he fell arse first into the river. Amid the scene in our minds of a raging torrent, he stood up and looked at us confused as the water only came up to his ankles.

"It's not deep at all, you liars," he wailed.

"Ah, shut up, you baby," I interrupted, "You ruined the whole thing. Now its just a stupid little stream again."

"Yeah, we may as well just go home," added Skip.

Grace was looking very happy that she hadn't been picked to test the rope. At only eight years old, she was still going through the initiation process herself.

That was last year, and if Tommy McGuire had been with us then, he would have known that the river was only ankle deep and he had nothing to fear. Of course, like Michael, he was gullible, and I could see the fear in his eyes as he contemplated crossing the wall bridge and possibly falling in. Michael didn't let on that he knew the truth. He knew what Tommy was going through, but he now knew what the fun of being on the other side of the joke felt like.

"Do you think we'll get caught?" Tommy asked.

"Well, you won't if you're able to run faster than the massive vicious dog the gardener has patrolling the grounds," Skip answered; catching on to the game Mary was playing.

We loved to tease the ignorant and innocent. If they couldn't come up with their own adventures and always begged to tag along on ours, then they deserved a little teasing, and we deserved a little fun.

"Why, will he bite me?" Tommy asked, really looking scared this time.

"Rip your head off is more like," I joined in. This was starting to be fun, and it was keeping my mind off the woods and the memories inside.

"Well shit, then I'm going home," he said, and began to turn around and go back.

"You're an awful bloody eejit, Tommy," Mary said in disgust. "Can't you tell that we're only messing with you?"

"Yeah, I knew it all along. I was only having you on myself," he answered.

"Sure you were, and if I believe that one, then I'll believe anything," Mary responded.

We were quiet for a while then, as we entered the trees by the sewage treatment plant. It was simple to enter the Secret Wood, but getting out quickly in a blind panic was trickier. My stomach was in knots, and I was trembling slightly as I set foot in the place I vowed never to return to. The wood seemed dark and sinister, the air heavy and smelling of decay, and the trees closed in all around me, blocking any escape. My breath came in gasps as my heart rate increased, and terror once again seized control of my mind. It took all of my willpower not to turn and run.

Why had I gone with him? Why hadn't I listened to my mother and stayed on the main road? If I had, nothing would have happened, and I would not have this horrible memory constantly lurking under the surface of my conscious mind, waiting for the opportunity to rear its ugly head.

It was a cold winter's day in February 1978, with snow on the ground, and I was walking out the main Cappa Road to meet up with Kathleen and Mary, who had gone out there ahead of me. It was a mile walk and one that I had done many times before, but always with someone else. I could tell that Mam had reservations about letting me walk that far by myself, and I begged her, promising that I would stay on the main road and go straight to Cappa. I was doing fine, walking along a low stone wall and jumping over the gaps in the wall where little footpaths led up a grassy knoll to brightly painted benches for people to sit on. As I cleared the last gap and landed perfectly on the other side, I saw him watching me on the footpath a little further ahead.

"Where're you goin'?" he asked me in a friendly voice.

"To meet my sisters at Cappa," I answered, as I returned his smile.

"There's a short cut you know," he said.

"I know, but I promised Mam that I would take the main road because I'm on my own."

"If you come with me then you won't be alone anymore, and we can go the short cut way and get there much quicker," he lied to me as nice as can be, and I was a stupid eejit to believe him.

He was in his late teens or early twenties, and I considered him my friend. He often bought me sweets, and I had been invited into his house by his mother to hold and cuddle the kittens her cat had had. So, naturally, I thought that his idea was a great one, and I eagerly agreed to it, much to my sorrow every day since.

"Let's go back into town and I'll buy you an apple, and then we'll head out the old Fort Road," he suggested.

"Okay," I agreed.

"Why don't you send your dog home?" he asked.

"Her name is Darky and she's not my dog, she's a stray and she's been following me all day. She's very attached to me. I'm taking care of her."

"Well, try to shoo her home anyway. We'll be faster without her."

I tried to shoo Darky away, but she kept coming back with a smile on her face and her tail wagging a mile a minute. So she came along with me and was by my side as I fled a short while later.

After buying me the apple, he walked me down Moore Street to Stewart Street, which led us to the Fort Road at the top of the hill on the way out to Kilimer. As we walked up the hill, he changed his mind and told me that my way was better after all, and we should cross the field and cut through the small wood to get back onto the main road again. I secretly felt proud that he thought my way was better, and so I took off into the field after him. When we entered the wood next to the sewage treatment plant, I began to feel a little uneasy. We had just walked in one big circle, and if I had stayed on Cappa Road, I would be in Cappa already. Now we were heading back to the very spot we had started from. This didn't make any sense to me. I looked at the little dog, and her hackles were up and she was growling a low growl, deep in her throat. The sun wasn't shining in this part of the wood. It was dark, cold, and creepy, and everything was still. No birds were singing. The sewage plant was empty and silent and surrounded by a fence. A high stone wall ran along one side of the wood and the small river along the other side. We had entered in the one spot where there wasn't a fence, a wall, or the river.

He stopped in a small clearing between the trees and asked me if I wanted to play a little game. I remembered the game we used to play, and I felt too old for such a silly game now, so I told him no. He grabbed me from behind and started to thrust himself against me. The little dog began to bark furiously.

"Shut up, you mangy bitch," he yelled at her.

"She's not mangy," I yelled back. "Let me go."

I struggled and squirmed to break free, and as I turned my head back to see what he was doing, I saw something sticking out of his pants. Now, I had seen Skip's before in the bathtub, and I had asked my mother what it was, and she told me that it was what made boys and girls different. I accepted that answer and never gave it another thought until that day when I saw it in a different way. I knew something very wrong was happening, and I began to struggle even more. After managing to worm my way out of his arms, I ran like hell. Fear began to build up inside of me. If he caught me, what would he do? He wouldn't want anyone to know what had happened. It was dark and very secluded among the trees, and no one knew where I was. Why had he lied about taking me to Cappa? He never intended to take me there at all. What did he intend to do with me? As the fear grew, I was able to run faster and faster.

"If you don't stop, I'm going to kill your dog," he yelled after me.

I looked back and could see the little dog running to catch up with me. Had she tried to slow him up? Did she bite him? I couldn't find the easy way out but ran instead along the fence to the stone wall. I was trapped. Then I saw a high, spiked, red, metal gate. Looking back one last time, I saw him gaining on me as he struggled to zip up his fly, cursing and out of breath. The little dog was at my feet, and bending down, I grabbed her by the scruff of the neck and threw her up and over the gate. I leaped up and began to frantically climb over it myself. When I jumped down on the other side, I slipped on the snow and fell over and could hear the gate rattle as he began to climb after me. I jumped to my feet and began to run towards the low wall with the gate but realised that if he went left to the bridge, he could cut me off on Stewart Street. I ran for the bridge, moaning and sobbing all the way across the field, over the bridge, and up the street to my house.

I never saw the little dog again. She was my companion during the worst ordeal in my life, and I believe that maybe she was my guardian angel in disguise. I know that he didn't hurt her because he never stopped running after me, and I saw him turn off down the lane by the slaughterhouse when he realised that he wasn't going to catch me.

I didn't have the words to describe to my mother what had happened, so I told her that he had flashed me. I saw a look of fear in her eyes, and she began to ask me all kinds of questions. The more questions she asked the more confused and frightened I became. I was beginning to blank out what had happened, and it all became fuzzy and unclear. All I wanted was to be held close and told that everything would be all right, but instead her eyes ran up and down my body to see if he had done anything else to me. She was horrified at what could have happened to me and relieved that I had not been raped. The effect on me was traumatic nonetheless.

When my father came home, he held me gently at arms length with both hands on my shoulders and looking me in the eyes, he asked me to tell him what had happened. I just wanted to go to my room and hide. I was shutting down inside. My initial fear had turned into anger, and that is the emotion I expressed to my father. He did not witness the fear that I struggled to suppress. My trust had been shattered, my innocence blown to smithereens, and my sense of security was stolen from me forever. I looked at men differently from that day on, and it was a long time before I could sit on my father's lap and feel comfortable. I used to love his hugs and cuddles and the way he threatened to kiss a hole through the side of my head, but after that day and for months to follow, I inwardly cringed whenever he touched me. I never told him, though, because I didn't want to hurt his feelings. It wasn't his fault, after all.

I went to my room and curled up in a ball on top of the blankets and rocked myself back and forth. I had cried all of my tears; only dry sobs came now. As I rocked, I began to remember all the other times when Peter had done something similar to me. He had taken me behind the church then, but I didn't know what he was doing, and I hadn't seen anything. He called it a game. Tossing some coins on the grass, he would pick me up from behind bending me over at the waist. He told me to try to grab as much of the coins as I could while he bounced me up and down. Whatever I was able to grab, I could keep. I didn't know then, but after what I saw in the wood I knew what that bastard was really doing, and I felt dirty, stupid, and oh so angry.

The fog slowly closed over my consciousness, and I fell into a deep, black void of sleep where no rest was had. Later that evening, I came downstairs to the kitchen. When I entered, I saw Kathleen, Mary, and Grace all sitting around the table with Mam and Dad talking about me, and I was asked to tell them what had happened. I was so embarrassed and ashamed, and I was beginning to think that it was my fault. I had disobeyed Mam after all. It was hard for me to talk about it, and I don't remember saying a word. I don't remember much of the days and weeks that followed, only that I thought everyone in town knew, and I didn't want to go outside.

The *Gardai* were notified as well as the parish priest. No charges were brought up against him on the premise that he would submit to psychiatric evaluation and care, which he did. My parents watched me like a hawk for weeks afterwards to see how badly I was affected and were relieved when my perky self emerged once again. I did resume normal living, but the memory of that day never wandered too far from my mind. It was never mentioned again, except when Dad told me that forgiveness was the only way I would be able to get past what had happened to me. I needed to forgive and forget. I tried. I said that I did forgive him, and I desperately tried to wipe that day from my memory, but just when I thought it was gone, it would poke its filthy head up and jeer at me.

Here I was now, reliving the whole bloody thing again. Luckily, the wood was small, and it didn't take long to get to the wall bridge. We showed Tommy how to cross, and when we were all on the other side, we made our way to Bonnie Dune's orchard. Her property was surrounded by a low barbed wire fence, which we very carefully ducked under as Mary held the barbed wire up. Skip held it up for Mary to duck under, and then there we all were in the orchard with apple trees galore to choose from. I picked the one closest to me and like a monkey scaled the branches to the top of the tree. I opened the plastic bag I had tied to the belt of my trousers and began to pick apples and drop them in. When I looked around, I saw Mary, Skip, Grace, Michael, and Tommy busy doing the same thing. We were so engrossed in the work at hand that we didn't hear the breaking of twigs or the rustle of underbrush as the gardener slowly approached from the direction of the house.

"What are ye brats doing here?" his voice boomed into the silence.

I jumped out of my skin.

"Get down here this minute or I'll call the *Gardai*," he ordered.

We quickly climbed down to the ground, and dropping the bags of apples we had worked so hard to collect, we ran towards the barbed wire fence and freedom. If we could make it over the wall bridge and through the wood before getting caught, we'd be all right. As I squirmed under the wire, my long blonde hair got tangled in the barbs, and I didn't wait to untangle it but rather left a good clump of hair hanging in the breeze. It would make excellent forensic evidence if Bonnie Dune decided to press charges. Being that we didn't get away with any of her apples this time, she didn't have much of a case against us except trespassing, and that was a minor offence. It was déjà vu all over again as I ran through the wood and across the field toward the bridge.

When we reached the bridge, we looked back and saw that no one was following at all. Relief swept over us, and we began to laugh and giggle.

"Well, there'll be no apple tarts this time, Skip," I said.

"Yeah, and I was so looking forward to a grand slice with a cup of tea," he replied. "I bet Bonnie Dune will use the apples we picked to make herself a fine tart."

She probably would have if Bonnie Dune were a real person. I learned years later that Bonnie Dune was the name of the house and grounds, and I haven't a clue who it was that lived there.

"Well, at least we're not in jail," Tommy said, and I could see the look of relief on his face. I think that we all felt relieved that we weren't being dragged at that moment to the *Garda* barracks for questioning.

"I'm going home," Tommy added, as he went over to where we had hid his bike in the bushes.

Now, I don't know why we didn't just lift his bike over the low wall next to the gate down the field a bit where we had gotten it in. Instead, like complete eejits, we decided to lift it up and over the bridge. Tommy stood on top of the fence, Mary and Skip lifted the bike up to him, and he lifted it up to me. I was standing on top of the wall, and I pulled it up and then placed it carefully down on the road. As I straightened back up after putting the bike on the road, I wobbled and lost my balance and fell backwards off the bridge and into the river. Mary best described what happened next when I heard her tell the story to Kathleen that night.

"She lost her balance and fell backwards into the river. She twisted in mid-air, and when she landed in the water on her hands and knees, she, quick as lightening, jumped back out again and landed on the bank. It was like fast motion in a film, and I swear that she didn't even get wet. Not one little drop. It was so amazing! I have never seen anyone move so fast in my life. It was like something you'd see on the telly."

She was right. I didn't get wet at all. It was, with cat-like reflexes that I jumped back out of the water, and when I stood on the bank of the river, my clothes were dry as a bone. There must have been glass on the riverbed because the pointer finger on my right hand was badly cut, and so was my right knee. I climbed back up on the fence and over the bridge again, and by now I had had enough and just wanted to go home. As I walked up Stewart Street, the blood dripped from my hand and ran like rivulets down my shin and into my sock. When I passed Cuggernan's house, Mrs. Cuggernan came running out waving her arms in the air.

"Jaysus, she's split, she's split, the child is split," she cried.

"I'm fine, it's just a scratch," I said.

Mrs. Cuggernan was a lovely woman and the mother of my friend Mary. She was kind and loving with a constant smile upon her face. It was she who taught me one day how to iron a man's shirt and trousers. I was watching her iron at her kitchen table then, and she explained to me what she was doing and the tricks to getting the creases just right. I never forgot that lesson, much to my father's delight when he discovered what I had learned. I should never have told him, because he further explained how to get military creases down the front of a pair of trousers. He had served in the American Army and Air Force. On many an occasion since, when I'd be going upstairs to my room, I would see on the banister in the landing a pile of his trousers for me to iron.

"What happened, lovey?" Mrs. Cuggernan gently asked me, as she wrapped my hand in a hanky from her pocket.

"I fell off the bridge into the river," I answered, dangerously close to tears.

"But you're not wet," she was quick to point out.

"I know, isn't it brilliant?" said Mary. "She landed straight in the water and came out dry."

"It's a miracle," Mrs. Cuggernan agreed.

"More like dumb luck," I muttered, under my breath.

I was physically, mentally, and emotionally exhausted by now, and without saying another word to anyone I walked on home. The final adventure of my summer holidays was over, and it had been more than I bargained for. Sensing that I was upset, and thinking that it was only about getting caught and then falling off the bridge, Skip came up to me and offered me a lovely, big, green juicy apple from one of his pockets. He had stuffed his pockets and shirt with apples before putting any in his bag. The rest of us had filled our bags first and never did get to put any in our pockets. So, Skip came away with enough apples for each of us to have two. It wasn't a complete waste of time after all.

As I munched on my apple, enjoying its tangy juice, I thought it was silly to let the memory of one bad day ruin my life, and I vowed to either overcome the fear, or else bury it so deep inside of me that it would be forgotten forever. It would become a scar just like the ones that would form on my finger and knee, and I could live with scars. Little did I know that a wound like that never formed a scar. It would fester deep within and eventually find its way out to unconsciously affect decisions I would make in the future. What did a thirteen-year-old know about stuff like that?

When I got home, Mam wrapped my knee and finger in a bandage. I thanked her and resting my head on her chest, I closed my eyes and gave her a gentle hug. In the comfort and security of my mother's arms, I was a young and innocent little girl. I wished I could stay there forever. However, I was a teenager now and starting secondary school in three days. It was time to grow up. The summer holidays were over and, as they came to an end, so did my childhood.

Epilogue
Dropping the Stone

As we journey through our lives from infancy to old age, we are wounded by others and wound others in return in our humanness. This is life. Some of our past woundings are big and some are little, and many are traumatic to the psyche of our inner child. We learn to bury the wounding as a method of escaping the pain of remembering. We make decisions and develop behaviour patterns, which enable us to prevent issues and emotions of the past from surfacing. The body never forgets, however, and the memory of each and every wounding is stored in the muscles and tissue throughout the body. Over time, these memories become dis*ease* as we are no longer at *ease* with our own true selves.

Shamans, or spiritual healers, use the analogy of the *Bowl of Light*, which represents the brilliance of our soul or spirit at birth. Gradually as others wound us, these woundings become stones and accumulate inside our bowl of light, and over time the light is dimmed. For some of us it is a tiny spark waiting to be uncovered.

Rev. Dr. J.C. Husfelt of The Morning Star Institute, on his web page www.divinehumanity.com, teaches us how to begin to drop the stones through forgiveness and letting go.

Forgiveness can be given and the issues/emotions (stones) connected with them from the past can be released. Focus your intent on the forgiveness and the wounding (issue/emotion) you want to release. *Always take just one wounding at a time, and begin slowly with just a small wounding from the past—metaphorically, just a little pebble!*

Find a stone in nature and ask permission with your mind to use it.

Then take the stone and sit with it alone (preferably in nature) and talk your emotions (tears, cry, shout, yell—whatever it takes) into this stone. You may only need to spend a few minutes doing this; then put the stone away in a special place, or you may even carry it with you. When you are ready to say more words of healing to the stone, repeat—as often as necessary. This process may take hours, days, weeks, or months (depending on the size of the stone). When you feel ready to release, visit a stream, lake, or ocean. It can be at any time of the day, but dawn or dusk symbolically is the best.

Sit by the water's edge and relax. More words may need to be said and more tears shed. When you are ready, Let Go, Forgive, and Release—drop (or toss) the stone into the water. As you let go of the stone, you are letting go of the stone within your Chalice of Light. If you are unable to open your fingers and release the stone, it just means that you have more work to do on this wounding. Keep the stone and take it back home with you. Repeat talking to your stone (can be silently in your mind). When you feel you are ready again, revisit the stream, lake, or ocean and release.

When you have forgiven and let go of this past wounding, sit by the water's edge and feel the lightness within you. Bless, give thanks, and leave an offering before you depart. Bless, thank, and love yourself for having the courage, wisdom, and love to forgive and let go.

As an apprentice of The Morning Star Institute, and with the guidance of Dr. Husfelt and his beautiful wife Sherry, I have been able to forgive and release many of the painful memories from my childhood. I had tried to bury them and, in doing so, I buried my inner child and silenced her. When I released the stones, not only did I feel lighter and brighter, but also I found my Irish child again. This book is her voice.

Glossary

Some of the words in this book are either in the Gaelic tongue, or they are slang words often spoken in Ireland. Here is an explanation of what they mean.

biscuits	cookies
bonnet	hood of a car or tractor
cheeky	being fresh.
cooker	stove
craic	fun.
dual carriageway	two lanes each way on a highway
eejit	idiot
Gardai	Irish Police Force
gobshite	another word for idiot
knackered	tired
loo	toilet or bathroom
lorries	trucks
Pure wah sham!	Wow!
quid	one pound note in Irish money
spanner	wrench
Yank	American
ye	you all

Works Cited

The following excellent books were used as sources for historical facts on Kilrush and the surrounding areas:

O'Brien, Sister Pius. *The Sisters of Mercy of Kilrush and Kilkee.* Printed by Clare Champion Printers in 1997.

Spellissy, Sean. *Clare, County of Contrast.* Published by The Connacht Tribune in 1987.

Printed in the United States
22388LVS00002B/32